Xmas Town

Spamerica's Demockery

Dr. Robert Blackman

"Xmas Town", Spamerica's Demockery, "The Arse of the Farce", is shackled to a revolving door in the center of town, where an army of suits from the lost and found, parade! It's a mosh pit like, mudslinging, body slamming wrestling match, overrun by a January 6th rabid mob of self criminalized, self emasculated, bibilism-tribalism white faced hydrophobic, xenophobic, homophobic tourists.

Pockmarked with rabbit holes, the ostrich like Con-us AKA Congress, plunge head first into the sand. The red eyed, scratched cornea, ***mashugana's*** swear on a stack of bibles, El Presidente Don T-Rump AKA Emperor Puffoon, won the erection, make hate, divisiveness and distrust, the centerpiece of Spamerica's Demockery, Repugnant Party.

Walled in by discarded Christmas trees, to the north is Canadastan to the southwest Mexiraq, two of Xmas Town's closest enemies. Discarded Christmas Trees are set on fire. Corpses of an overused holiday, burn unceremoniously. The bonfire to authoritarian totalitarianism celebrating isolationism and nationalism, in a rallying cry to nativism and tribalism. The chest beating, junkers are known as humanures, in a shit storming pileup.

Xmas Town has a pasty faced white patina surrounded by belching smoke stakes, plumbed with lead pipes, so the drinking water runs through made up recycled hogwash.

Xmas Town, Spamerica's Demockery has turned freedom into an uninvited jailbird, who lives on over washed platitudes and synthetic absurdities, showcasing "the demockery of democracy", a satirical rampaging, the Z movie of Z movies, plastered on Russian tanks as the "Z man" epitomizes, the ultimate zeitgeist of a fledgling, faltering new millennium, showcasing a doomsday escapades of a riot in calamitous Cirque Folies Bergere. "Xmas Town" with a circus like atmosphere, under the big flop, flopping around like a fish out of water, trying to blindly find the light at the end of the tunnel, in a maze of miscues and missteps, faux pas, flagrant debacles, as the global unraveling, exposes the fatuous grotesquely 'huge' underbelly of the 'blimpy puffoon', stay puft's orange dumbster (a portmanteau, dumpster and dumb combined; dumbster, dumbisms rather than Trumpisms), "a garbage in garbage out", weaponized narrative, January 6th, swarming hordes of Oaf Bleepers and Oy Goy's, storm the capitol, looking for the capitol lavatory, whipped into a frenzy by El Presidente Don T-Rump, who's claiming there is a cure, for the bent carrot syndrome and yes, he did win the 'erection', in a landslide, claiming to be huger than anyone else, while his army of certified rabid boner's, bear spray, defecate, assault, urinate, in what the Repugnant party calls “Legitimate Political Discourse”.

What appears to be a cult of personality, Emperor Puffoon AKA El Presidente Don T-Rump’s ass kisser’s, make a pilgrimage to Mired Pharsgo, to kiss the ring of "Emperor Puffoon", his lubricated 9 iron used as a way of members of the Repugnant party elite, self shaft obsequiously.

Like a symbolic stampede of elephants and donkeys, colliding head-on, the junk mania, crash course in self obliteration, gains traction.

It's become a socio-political shit house; Headbangers vs. Deadheads, throwbacks to The proverbial shit storm hit the fan and the fecal spatter has turned Xmas Town a ghostly white. The existential thread has poked the eye of the needling, rhetorical shyster, crap-box hyperbole. Exposing the garish, insufferably arrogant, Emperor Puffoon and his mob of humanure John's, the Pandora box rejects, overdosing on self serving junk. Another words, there are no words to describe, the scatology of goofball slinging, mud-wrestling in real time, in the public mosh pit. The capitol latrine and knuckle headed humanures, smear campaign, goes viral. The pissing contest has the humanures, a sub specious primate invertebrate; "thug slugs" storming the slippery slope of self aggrandizement and the demockeries of demockery are hell bent on self termination and annihilation. Constitutionally unsound, they shred any evidence of credibility and shove it into a sock draw, with Monica Lewinski's blue dress.

Xmas Town, with a backdrop of skyscrapers toppling, capitalism burns in effigy, while two unsung heroes, file a class action suit against El President "Crooked Don". T-Rump, They are defending the Native people, the Manhattoes, who were forcibly removed from their homes, at the southern tip of Xmas Town AKA Spamerica (which was once known as the island of Manhattan). El Presidente "Crooked Don" T-Rump has claimed eminent domain. He has had the Manhattoes moved to the northern end of Spamerica AKA Xmas Town, to the shanty town of Albya, which recently was hit by a devastating. 8.5 earthquake and a tsunami. Xmas Town AKA Spamerica refuses to help the Manhattoes. As the bonfire burns and the belching smoke stacks send soot and ash into the air, Xmas jingles continue to play ad nauseum.

seaturtlenation@gmail.com

Table of Contents

seaturtlenation@gmail.com

Xmas Town

Xmas Town is a cure-all fr the bloated crap shoot, sucker puncher! The vile, pile of liquored up guile, is his strong suit. Drunk on it, drugged on it. He knows he can beat any rap! He is the devil's poster demon. He is the embodiment of rank mediocrity. Art is his nemesis. Poetry is his neutralizer. The king of tom-foolery, enthroned on a fools-gold toilet, lathered in lavish Bullshit, code name, BS -2, Stooge of Con-Us (FYI Congress), CMS (Constitutional Muggers Scumbags) 666, owned by Jarhead Cushy, a Mid-Spamerica's (once Mid-Manhattan) acquisition. His "Cushy mushy" effective, status symbol, a financial money pit, ate his contract during a fit of buyer's remorse. What has been described as an CMS-666 (Constitutional Muggers Scumbags), overpriced schlock store, he meets in T-Rump Tower, for a glory hole, hump the junk, a back channel, junk U$A (Unholy State of Apathy), for a golden shower dossier rewrite. A Moscow porn flick starring none other than the tidy whitey and his Horny Stormy blowup, in homage to all women, including the first lady and Lady Liberty. The boot licking, lip service, jerk off try trafficking "Crooked Don's", "unholy bible of blabber".

Shoving his junk, down the throats of both whore-houses of Con-Us, King "Pimp" Con AKA Crooked Don, junk bludgeons his genuflexing, binary black and QQ (Queer and Quacked)! A tsunami whitewashed playbook, "The Farce of The Fleece", written by "Vlad the Impaler" (AKA Putin) a Napoleonic sized piroshki, filled with blood soaked Nemtsov memorabilia, sticking it to his marionette, the grim reaper puppeteer, spearfishing his catch of the millennium, El Presidente "Crooked Don" T-Rump. Bamboozled, hoodwinked, figuratively drawn and quartered, his majesty, from his oval pigpen lock box does ugliest ogre, prima facie balls and ass junk tower cover up as his minions do his bidding in a meeting of "The Slime". CMS-666 (Constitutional Muggers Scumbags), gives him a "get out of jail card" in a lackey's showing of gutless wonders, "John's gang banging that moneymaker, bombshell blonde".

As his portrait gets uglier and his face gets redder, his balls and ass speak, speaks volumes. "The Commander in Tweets", hogs, junk news. He feeds on his own garbage, while regurgitating tribal deadheads.

In his unlike Tennyson, "The Wreck of The Wreck", he crashes and burns dailies, splash across headlines. News becomes a transaction rewrite by what can be described as Machiavelli's ugly twin. Lying is his blood sport. Kill the messenger. Murder the truth. Sub clinical pathology grotesquely distorts. Ground hog day repeats ad infinitum. Pigged out on his brand, he wallows in his own vomit. Whitewashing his wreckage, the sociopath wants blind obedience.

Constitutionally unsound, he flogs the founding father's first line of defense. Calling the press, "The enemy of the people", he euthanizes freedom. He cuts out her heart, eviscerates the soul and bashes her unconscious, making her unrecognizable. A QQ (Queer Quacked) cutout, *Kristallnacht,* reincarnated-thuggery goes viral. BS-2 is QQ's Grand Wizard. As he stomps around the stage, in a braggadocio reenactment of the Fuhrer's Oz!

Fragile and broken, he makes good on his empty promises. His controller pulls his strings in a bitch slapping display of cold blooded, ruthless power and greed.

He continuously, rewrites and redefines his cartoonish redundant assault. Walled into to a lightless pathway to interment, he lashes out in retaliation.

A postural platform is backed by an inviolable trust, engaging in the valence of wholeness. It's the modern day alchemy, neutralizing the benign, innocuous poisons, that go unseen, out of earshot, insidiously hidden, in between the lines, slipping through the cracks; wanton apathy and near sighted complacency. Bringing us, a landmark allegory, a symbolic meandering, through the pages of Xmas Town.

Xmas Town allows for a moment to moment, collaboration, reinventing an internal dialogue, which calls for invoking an autonomous, self-determined, self - empowered subscription to resilience. Xmas Town is an infusion of our unexplored disbelief. That is our 99.9% of who and what we are. It is an unknown. Xmas Town presents us with the keys that make possible our deliverance, from the finite, short lived, instant fix, par boiled mediocrity, we define as a lifestyle. It is fundamentally unsound. Constitutionally unfit. BS-2, "The Stooge" is sucked off by a John whose alias is "Rocket Man". And in his "Tidy Whitey" auto-fellatio of a brutal, murderous thug goes viral. The "axis of trivial", also includes none other than, Vlad the Impaler. The world stage becomes the, "world's funny farm", where normalizing crazy gets to be the lynchpin to cyberspace crazier, graduating to unprecedented craziest.

While U. S. A. (Unholy Swamp of Apathy), to his or her detriment, over schedules and overbooks. Utilizing the overuse, insurance policy, they buy into assuring what is considered safe and normal. It is a mold, cast in stone; a steely, caged, close proximity, to pending violence, paralleled by a medical, invasive violation and prescribed toxic overload, driving the addicted abuser, into a frenzied, fever pitch ravenous, insatiable appetite, to do more, therefore, the need to do more is linked, to our subconscious, causing, a pathological ballooning hairdo, dyed ammonia colored white hate, turns matter (as in brain) cirrhosis black. Livid, galled ego-tramp, man-whore, trysts, gets his kicks, but can't kick the habit as he mounts, Ms. Junkyard Dog, in his hush money, moneymaker, misogyny to anyone claiming to be a woman.

BS-2 lost the popular vote, in a landslide rape artist bloodsucking hardcore betrayal.

A metronome monotone run by a head bowed, to a handheld pathway to toxic mediocrity. Out sourcing individuality, freedom is compromised. It becomes bound and tethered, to a bandwidth, the algorithms, mathematically, encircling an exponential controlling mechanism that you are tethered to. As we sacrifice our personal freedom, we become enslaved, by the devolution, switching from self-authored, self-directional motivation, to over-riding, eclipsing syntax, a silent, but deadly engineered, equation, one dimensional over-consumption

This exacting formulation, accelerates aging, by repositioning our time line, moving through a window of constraint and limitation, the technological omnipresence,

saturates our conscious mind and incrementally sets up a disconnect between the heart and brain, disengaging from an instinctual, innate wisdom, eclipsing circadian cosmic entrainment, with a finite, pending obsolete, manufactured self-imposed

calendared mousetrap, locked into a sequential fast track, a mechanistic gatekeeper, so we can manipulate and control, over thinking, without feeling the exhaustive redundantly unflattering rat race, we find ourselves, prescribing to, which habitually promotes degenerative disease processes, so like moths drawn to the flame, we burn out, in the overheated, toxic atmosphere, laden with competing fiber optic elements, surging through the same hardwired redundancy, the encrypted devices, continuously program and reprogram, a synchronicity, based on structured institutional priorities, tracking consumers, shuffling implement, living in the forecast, reconnoitered positioned, pinpointing our whereabouts, specifically designed around the feeding tube, dissemination of preprogrammed facts and simulated information. So our freedom becomes like a vestigial organ, an appendage which has, lost its usefulness, in a world, padlocked to its predisposed lifestyle.

The polluted biosphere, ominously pervades, looming insidiously, society's deadlocked, circumscribed time line, is riveted to a plethora of BS- 2 junk, throwing his balls and ass against 'the wall' and whatever sticks is the trick, he turns into megalomania.

His clatter is pernicious chatter, poisons his self-serving sucker punching wordy shit storm. The well of both houses, siphons off the scum of his mental masturbating egomaniac nuclear firestorm. It tends to over stimulate, the heart and brain, so what emerges is a manacled "numb dumb or the devolved BS-2 "humanure". A faceless brand of neo-Nazi, lily white transparencies, on the outside, a black empty pit on the inside, while mouthing a "right to be white", binary, black lives don't matter, in a whitening, one dimensional shit hole.

Forceps delivered wannabe's, subsisting in the shadow of BS-2, the stooge of Con-Us, CMS-(Constitutional Muggers Scumbags) 666. The knotted up ball of wax, melted into figurines, sucking up to BS-2, so they could win his approval. Sycophants bloodsucking lived on plagiarized untruths, "wall-ware bots", walled in by walling up their one dimensional hate surge, feeding off the genesis of an out of print, what they consider their "good book". Bible huggers, the metal of their muzzle, locked and loaded they are the offspring, genetically wired Emmett Till killers.

The collective brain trust was DOA when it came to policy. Water boy's to, King Con de Sade AKA 'Crooked Don', quarterbacking what is devolving into a nuclear holocaust, had them kneeling, on their knees in homage to botching, self-crotch dismemberment. The behemoth Hill was like a giant termite mound as they ate through the deadwood, into tapioca colored walls. Wall-ware bots institutionally driven by fear, transmuted into humanures.

The writing was illegible, producing, nightmarish consequences. Always waiting for the next shoe to drop, they veer sharply right, in a rightly self-righteous Charlottesville Gestapo goose stepping, hatemongers, BS-2 spin cycle, A killing field like non other, gunning for each other, was a second amendment, set in stone, take a bullet for each other. It wasn't exactly a love fest. It looked more like a suited up bunch, who claim to legislate, but more often bait and switch as they steal each other's thunder in a rogue's gallery of fake and blunder. Con-Us, CMS-666 (Constitutional Muggers Scumbags) legislate, in a static freeze frame, repeat histories failures, a wall-ware BS-2 police state brings into light the resurgence of neo-idiocy.

A sinister invasion, hooked up to the MDM (Medical Doping Model), invades and preempts, our natural ability to combat disease. Like a Cyclops El Presidente "Crooked Don" T-Rump, looks through his orbital implanted crystal ball and sees walls with no bridges. He scales 'the wall' and throws babies out with the bath water multiple times. This is no laughing matter. It's a wall to wall blockade. BS-2's hostile takeover, raiding those seeking shelter from the storm and dismisses their request for asylum and just throws them to the wolves. The wolves, Guccifer 2.0, decked out in wall-ware, hack the DOJ (Department of Jerk-offs), headed up by BS-2 sucker punching gospel doubling down on bellicose, red meat, bigot suspicion, noxious fear and institutional hate, hating anyone, who doesn't have the skin color of a Benjamin.

The moral equivalence has "the fat cat's" whorehouses mimicking a Kremlin suburb as Vlad the Impaler, screws them all with a nod and a wink, hell's stinky little tyrant, colludes, invades, corrupts, like a tyrannical puppeteer, he pulls BS-2 FYI Crooked Don's MLPD (Multiple Liar's Personality Disorder) strings, violently goes through an identity crisis, more hate, a xenophobic quagmire he sinks, into his oval shaped swamp, walled in by the overshadowing, ominous shroud of a nonexistent moral compass, which has turned him into a contemporary, Benedict Arnold.

Hooked up to a grid, CMS-666, cattle prods, the overzealous humanures, shock waves them, keeping them incessantly busy, overworked, overused restraints, overtired, dehumanized and desensitized. Our censored, politically correct repository has them scampering to the moral high ground of self-righteous hypocrisy.

The tightly occluded airwaves of their societal stranglehold, struggles to catch it's breathe. Breathing room is marginalized. There is no rest for the busied out humanures. Old habits, like a gun and a needle deliver the proverbial magic bullet. The numbing, deadening unfeeling, unforgiving tiredness, cuts to the bone. That aching exhaustion kills.

Xmas Town infuses the rejection of our failures, with a new found window, which opens the door, to an undiscovered dreamscape as it reroutes, our basic values of right and wrong. Forced to look at, why we lose our footing, in the "real world" and fall into, the abyss of loss, it permeates and soaks into, every pore of our being. It challenges us, to change, suffusing, the heart and mind, with a coalescing system; restoring innervation and self-motivation.

BS-2 kisses ass for brand and self-aggrandizement! God and country has been supplanted with not having 'the foggiest', only a crass, classless, contrived, smoke screen, "witch hunt", aberrational collusion and obstruction of justice is his swamp gruel like porridge, BS-2 and his groveling John's CMS-666 (Constitutional Mugger Scumbags), ram down the throats, red meat, cannibalistic, carnivore institutionalized QQ (Queer Quacked) 'Repugnant' lemmings.

It's his self-serving business model. As he holds hands with hell's stinky little tyrant and schmoozes and smooches with his favorite pandering murderous, thug ruler, a pudgy fratricidal maniac.

Xmas Town, parlays our mistakes, into a fertile accounting of where we've gone wrong, so we can deconstruct our believable, renegotiating the unbelievable continuum, which ignites, the fires of our passions. Circumventing the hollowness of success, based on material possession, a buttressed, propping up of an ego driven, linear accumulation of stuff, over scheduled, over bought, over exercised, overused, overtired and exhausted profile of a pinup lifestyle, rides on, the padded shock waves of our bodies and minds disconnecting, riding the gravy train, until it crashes and burns as the terror of jobless disenfranchisement, embodies the satanic ritual of BS-2 economic downturn as he shit-cans the USA (Unholy Swamp of Apathy).

The rush of doing and redoing, in a looped litany of things to do, from laundry, to nails and hair, the list, viciously cyclically recycles "more of the same", in a digitized, technological maelstrom, the gismos calendared, ticking time bomb are set to implode without warning, in a symptom based, diagnostic breakdown, based on an MDM (Medical Doping Model).

It's wrapped in the airtight alibi, an unbending negation, rigidly employed by the 'humanures', pigeonholed amplitudes, busied out opportunists, who navigate the one dimensional panoply of invisible mail, an armored reality, propped up by a concrete, impervious safety net, a cyberspace junket, faster and faster, the gigabyte power source, traveling at the speed of darkness, while refracted light permeates, the programmed allocation of a radioactive gridlock, predictably cordoned off, by a barbed wired lock down, chain linked, fenced in, wall-ware has taken over the airwaves, invaded cyberspace, in a walled off, shutdown, dragging around the ghostly wreckage, hitting a wall, the scrawled headlines describes pending destitution, while BS-2 torches the constitution, rapes Lady Liberty, at the same time bragging how, “My House Branded IS Where I Stand!!”

seaturtlenation@gmail.com

INTRODUCTION
© 2021RB

Xmas Town is a daredevil's play land, a risk taker's precipitous, high flying act into the boundless, far flung reaches of the unthinkable. It's before time and before god, that the unexplored steppes, unfounded and unseen, become the birthplace of a supreme player, who claims his birthright in an ageless celebration, to his unrecorded origin: Play.

This book is written in a new language, an internal dialogue, with a spellbinding, cutting-edge. There is magic here, unspoken and unsaid. The hammer strikes the anvil. A beveled edged sword is like the quill of a word-smith's playbook. It frolics and romps, jumps and leaps into the undiscovered, into a wonderland, fashioned into a prismatic interplay.

Ride the wave, a lyrical madness, with no measured limitation. Our surfboard playbook is in the pipeline, just ahead of the curve, a curling, foaming, roaring, immeasurably cacophonous, briny, cresting silence.

The major characters are Ungohdt and Dohg. They are like Siamese twins, joined at the hip. The biped claims to be Ungohdt from "Ungohdt's House of Disbelief, embodying the disenfranchised amorphous reclamation of being and not being. Predating the cosmos, it is simply called "non". Dohg, a floppy eared pukka, sprung from the prehensile tail of Ungohdt, a quadruped, who continually questions Ungohdt every step of the way, but there is an unspoken love, between the

two of them. An indescribable affection, undefined and unimaginable is their bond.

Two unsung heroes, Ungohdt and Dohg, seem to appear at of nowhere, at the southern tip of an island, known as Xmas Town AKA Spamerica. They are there primarily, to help the native people, the Manhattoes. They are the indigenous people, who settled on their island centuries ago. They have been kicked off their land, given a few trinkets and handed eviction notices. Claiming eminent domain, El Presidente "Crooked Don" T-Rump is poised, in a hostile takeover. The racketeers and profiteers of Wall Street, the ruling power, demanded that they leave. The tyrants of commerce, driven by insatiable greed, had no idea, what was about to happen.

Ungohdt is having not the remotest connection to any of the gods of the humanures, who were devolved from humans. As a matter of fact, even though he has come to Spamerica, reincarnated as a vagabond with his Dohg, he repudiates any connection to anthropomorphic gods (made in the image of man). Ungohdt and Dohg first made their appearance at the tip of Manhattan, at ground zero.

The twin towers, mega giant behemoths, like lumbering "buysauruses", toppled over, when struck by a gigantic ticking time bomb. The steel girders, glass and concrete crumbled under the irrepressible heat of futility. The gridlocked infrastructure, society's skyscraper, rectangular rubrics, swayed, creaked and crackled and then with the gasping irony of time immemorial it slowly dissolved.

The big bang theory had been redefined. On an unavoidable collision course, a proverbial, ticking time bomb flew into the proverbial brick wall, but this time, there was concrete evidence of its existence. The existential threat of pending doom materialized. The impossible was actualized.

On impact the explosiveness, caused an unstoppable chain reaction. The gateway to our temporal reality was demolished. A cataclysmic breakdown ensued.

Happenstance ran amuck. The preservation of the species was threatened. A war of attrition, played out. Like confetti in a doomsday parade, the playwright shredded this unwritten chapter.

A floating crap game, anchored to bedrock, zeroed out. What was left was a seemingly endless paper trail of death sentences, signed, sealed and delivered. Unknowingly, the number crunchers' huge margin of error had not been factored in by terrorizing, "errorists (the devolving of a "terrorist", into an errorist)". They packaged and repackaged, outsmarted and outdid, and connived and contrived methods of practicing gravy train economics (the rich get richer, the poor get poorer), bringing down the house before it ever fell. It was predestined and preordained. There was no shelter from the imperfect storm.

An inferno of flames and smoke licked and lapped at steel girders, the underpinning of a rocky foundation that found its doomsday without knowing. It wasn't on the calendar, it wasn't planned, no one was ready for what was about to happen.

The T-Rump brand is rubber stamped on the psyche of a world on plethora overload. His smirking, smug sardonic looking, pouting mouth, fake tan, dyed brows and bouffant hair sprayed comb over, is his frontal assault of a habitual megalomania blitzkrieg. Farcical, he oozes hypocrisy.

He has displaced indigenous people, starting with the island of Manhattan, in which Manhattoes were thrown off their land. Babies are ripped from mother's arms. A wall of disdain and flagrant racism, brick and mortar cultural divisiveness, has the house of cards deconstructing.

A power vacuum sucks the oxygen out of the radioactive, gridlocked atmosphere, igniting the firestorm, a conflagration like a mythical beast, awakens the invisible Kraken, devouring what was thought to be the unsinkable dual Titans of Commerce.

The devolution of Planet Earth to Plan-It-Kill went undetected. Overuse was a major killer. Addictions anywhere—from exercise to eating, from disease to dieting to war—are missed, misread and misunderstood. Humanures—plastered on junk, in a race against time, on a virtual reality treadmill—were strung out.

Killing was the operative. Whatever was targeted had to be killed. The painkiller was a laundry list of "need to do," and doing more and more of "need to do" things replicated killing. The busy drug was the classic painkiller.

They had not only fallen off the wagon, but the wagon had crashed and burned. The wreckage of the killing field was strewn with debris, the binging and boozing was now unstoppable. Bottled gods were guzzled, glassy eyed drunkards, drunk on the liquored up good book, liquid lunch of high octane jet fuel, found their mark and delivered their blindsided, knock-out blow. A shock wave reverberated. Airtime had hit critical mass. Zero degrees of separation, between opposing forces, collided and self-destructed. Inside traders were vaporized. The crap shoot of one million to one, actualized.

No one saw it coming. As the terror of terrors filled the skies with ash and smoke, billowing over the skyline, every waking moment was consumed by an event, which evoked terror.

It struck a nerve, as a matter of fact, every nerve in the cosmos, echoed with feared terror. And then terror, in some maddening, ironic way, turned into a product. Terror became the hottest product on the market. Its global reach has consumed the world, in the over-consumption of terror.

I.S.I.S. (Idiot Squad of Isolated Savages) with the help of El Presidente "Crooked Don" T-Rump, surreptitiously employed the numbing effects, to an audience of 'numb dumb', consumers. Terrorized humanures, were fattened up, for the overkill. Branding was no problem. T-Rump and I.S.I.S. invaded cyberspace. T-Rump's junk, spanned the beveled edged world, according to El Presidente "Crooked Don" T-Rump.

I.S.I.S. had infiltrated the floor of the stock exchange and was decapitating, corporate god-heads of industry by propagandizing the zealots hijacked religion

Harvesting the poppy fields of Canadastan, which borders Spamerica, to the north and west, Mexiraq to the south and east, were vying for this potential incredibly lucrative market.

I.S.I.S. (Idiot Squad of Isolated Savages) secretively, with Violentology, synthesized a highly addictive drug, smuggled across the border of Xmas Town. The ingredients were a combination of acetone and peroxide, with the residue gum from poppies as well as a mushrooming hybrid mold, which could manufactured into a white powdery substance. It was named Kihl.

It later surfaced that Kihl, was the drug of choice, developed by El Don Hubbub, founder of Violentology and author of Lianetics. In an implosive meltdown, internal war zone of incited terror, the brutally abusive nature of Kihl, anger had all the earmarking of a street drug, but with the global reach of the pharmaceutical houses, it was advertised as a “biologic”, giving El Don Hubbub license to enforce his teaching. It was a killing spree like none other, a painkiller overdose, promoting the Lianetics of Violentology.

Ungohdt at first, naively, but with great optimism, thought he would save what was once a verdant, fertile island, which was now in the tyrannical clutches of El Presidente "Crooked Don" T-Rump. He wanted to give back the land to the Manhattoe Indians and rewrite the peace treaty. But he soon realized how hopeless it seemed. It was a lost cause. So he embarked on starting his own company, based on conservation and preservation. Ungohdt brought with him, from the non-seeds. Ungohdt planted non-seeds where the twin towers once stood.

In a very short time (in months rather than years), a rain forest had miraculously grown. Giant, majestic non trees, reaching up to the sky, forming a canopy of, dense and seemingly impenetrable foliage, were now visible from space, in all their wondrous glory. Wildlife, especially the birds drawn to this marvelous rainforest with beautiful, colorful plumage, songbirds sung as the sun rose.

But still the greenhouse gases from the ongoing bonfire continued, flames licking and lapping against the night sky. Humanures continued to discard their trees, burning like a crematorium.

Ungohdt and Dohg had also planted a vegetable garden in the rich loam and mulch on the forest floor. Vegetables were amazingly large. Their dwelling was inside the trunk of a noble non tree. With a twenty-one meter diameter, this colossus served them well and provided them with shelter.

Ungohdt, had created a truly remarkable habitat, in a world that was mostly underwater. Manhattan was the only island left, in a part of the continent called Spamerica. Wall Street had crashed decades ago and was now all boarded up, like an abandoned wingless albatross. At one time it was the high-flying, big biz capitol, the Mecca for big-time movers and shakers. Those glory days were gone from the culture that had taken an irrevocable downturn, a downward spiral, exposing the underbelly of a gridlocked society, another layer in the one dimensional, episodic misadventure of greed and power.

Wall Street had made its final killing, but ironically, in its own misguided, misinformed, insufferable, egregious way, it collectively nose-dived into a pitiful, self-deconstruction. Ironically, 'the killing', had backfired. Dead in the water was the fragmented wreckage of its own house of cards. Its real estate had plunged into the murky, fathomless depths, devalued the presidency, in what had become whitey's house of ill-repute.

Brokered deal makers, flaunted fakers, prepackaged gold bricks smashed MS-666 "fat" cat house of glass. The idiomatic supposition, "The farce of the fleece", written by the phallic ghost of El Presidente "Crooked Don" T-Rump hit home when the gavel struck and the closing bell rang, like a death knell as the stoners on glazed donuts, bicarbonate of soda, Tums and fiendish caffeine junkies, were all lathered up for the unexpected doomsday tragedy. The glittery glass house hit rock bottom, shattering into a zillion pieces. The theater of folly had gone to black and the stock exchange had turned into a killing floor, littered with unsigned proxies of failed companies.

"Too Big To Fail" and "MISSION ACCOMPLISHED", were emblazoned across the helm of the sinking ship. The Titans of commerce, were about to go down and nothing and nobody could stop it. Ground zero became a graveyard. The acrid smell of death loomed. Reality became a frightening apparition. What had seemed normal and safe turned into inconsolable loss and despair. But out of the carnage there would be deliverance. Standing at the epicenter of that rebirth, was Ungohdt and his pukka, Dohg.

seaturtlenation@gmail.com

non

Before god there was non.
Before creation there was non.
non was not of thought,
…not of mind,
…not of heart,
…not of flesh,
it was not of spirit.
non was infinitely infinite
non cued silhouettes, in a sunless arabesque,
non in life, gave birth, to death
and in death, aborted life,
neither bore a resemblance to either,
only to non and both embraced harmony
and the inharmonious, choppy seas of adversity
and in a moonless night,
delivered a nightingale's melody.
non cradled, alone,
in the bough of a non tree,
alone had found sanctuary,
but lost its way,
a forest dweller,

a dreamer orphaned by a pendulum, alone wandered through non,
in an arbor of dichotomies,
wholeness, sanctified the mystery,
and paradoxes, interwove,
with zero degrees of separation,
bearing the fruit of enchantment.
non was before time,
non was not made of things,
there were no universes,
no galaxies, no stars,
no planets, no moons, only non.
non had the power of one.
like the surface of a still lake, mirroring,
non reflected.
A black gardenia is a black gardenia
as non is non.
non had no light nor darkness
nor shadow to cast.
non had no elements, such as fire
non was more, like an earthworm,
that wormed its way
through fallow fields,

in hollow gardens, where nothing grew. Nothing, from non, somehow became, non.

And then nothing, a legless passage, washed onto an unexplored shoreline,

a vast empty sea, unfounded emptiness,
a waterless soundless, nakedness,
as silent as a feather,
floating through space.
There were no discoverers of non.
Observers, had not yet, been observed.
But from non, a non-thinking,
a nonexistence bounded.
It was flightless. There were no footsteps echoing,
no footprints,
on a spiraling stairway…
made of obsidian sand, only the non.
The eternity of non,
was in its perfect stillness.
Unreason at the helm of the ship of non,
a ship without masts or rudder,
drifted in perpetuity, perpetuating non,
And so non in its nothingness

and emptiness, in a foundry of non-metallurgy, a die was cast.

A plowshare, like a chariot shaped cloud,
plowed through non,
leaving in its wake
a furrowed non, seeded Eden.
The steamy breath,
seen from the nostrils of wild horses
at the crack of dawn
in an appaloosa sky,
a herd migrated into non.

And the song of galloping hooves
danced along a canyon floor,
disappearing into a non-portal,
the door to non-ending,
rainbows in a translucent mist,
worn like a lacy shawl,
covered the face of sunrise.
In that moment of solitude,
the first question mark was born,
like the very first whorl,
to tell a tale of treeless, petrified forests.

Markers depicting starlight,

gleamed like black pearls.

A mark, in quotes, parenthetically assigned, was unreadable,

A fetal-positioned mark, found its cocoon,
in its infancy, innocence asked, in repose.
Resting on the wings of a monarch,
a horizon trembled.
The nectar of a blossom, gave sustenance.
What flowered? Who sustained?
For the first time in all non-creativity,
non had a chance to play,
chance evoked flexibility,
likened to swaying bulrushes
or tall palms, in a Saharan desert,
caught by the wind of chance,
in an otherwise, windless silence.
non became the provocateur,
shooting an arrow, from a long bow,
non's quiver had only one arrow,
and that was the one, solitary one,
hitting its target,
it resonated like a tuning fork.
A vibration in the key of non-summoned
Trumpeting, non-heralded nature,

whose womb,
harbored the continuum of play,
in a hushed rhapsodic melody,
a soundless, wordless mantra, helped birth.
Play engaged.
Fawn eyes and tiger stripes
and an elephant trunk,
chameleon in nature,
play did what play, naturally does.
In hides and horns,
dusks and skins
of upright listeners
and seers,
separating the firmament,
of a salmon, colored perigee,
from star burst nova's,
winnowed apogees.
of non-counting timelessness,
ripened kernels,
passed through,
a hand blown hour glass,

like lilting fireflies,
the symphony played,

forever and ever.
Play was the antagonist,
the absolute protagonist,
the ultimate thespian, an actor,
non acting, an artist, non-drawing
or sculpting, but nonetheless playing,
the inexhaustible player, tireless, reposed, pulling and pushing,
igniting energy, incipient energy,
playing its way through non.

An interplay, summoned
as the question mark
took shape and form
inside the belly of non.
Forged from the tinsel strength
of a field of wheat,
golden heads from
which wildernesses were seeded
played on.

seaturtlenation@gmail.com

Xmas Town

Chapters

seaturtlenation@gmail.com

Chapter 1: Ungohdt/Dohg Shootout

They just showed up. Coming out of nowhere, claiming to come from a nebulous unmapped place, called "non", Ungohdt and Dohg emerged. They also proclaimed that they were summoned by the indigenous people, Manhattoes, who lived on the island of Manhattan, now called Xmas Town AKA Spamerica,

Ungohdt's seminal, "great spirit", was very much akin to the Manhattoes and was known as "The Oogle Ogle Unboggler," appearing to be a cross between the Kokopelli and Harlequin. This magical being, was the embodiment of both, "the great spirit" and "the great mystery", inextricably bound to non. The Oogle Ogle Unboggler came through the great portal at the summit of Mount Whitney. Ungohdt and Dohg were its servants, only messengers, vagabonding on a path, ending up on the west side of what was once, lower Manhattan, that is, what was left of it. At what time, it was considered, the heart of the financial world. Where the follies of greed and power ruled, obfuscating their motives, driven by hoarding, coffers bursting with ill-gotten gains, the humanures devolved into lascivious lust that could never be satisfied.

An "Island of Hills," Manhattan was taken away from the aboriginals, the native people, the Manhattoes, who were the original residents of the island. They were determined, to restore the place, where devastation and incomprehensible destruction had occurred. They had let the sub-specious known as humanures—neck-tied, suited up rat racers—sack and loot, what was once, a pristine, natural habitat.

Manhattoe natives were hunters and gathers. When taking a life for food, whether fish or foul or wild game, they apologized to the animal and to mother earth and to the Oogle Ogle Unboggler. Oogle Ogle Unboggler manifested as Ungohdt/Dohg at the very site of where the twin towers stood. Monolithic, Titans of commerce that housed, on a given day, literally thousands of humanures.

Fully fueled, flying deathtraps, ticking time bombs struck these monumental edifices, with such force, that these skyscrapers, shook right down to their foundations. The reverberating, sound of an exploding death knell, struck like a nuclear missile, igniting the giant steel girded powerhouses, turning them into burning effigies. It was as if hell itself had reemerged on the southern tip of Manhattan. The blistering inferno, swallowed up the girded safety net and almost in slow motion, consumed everything in its path. An uncontainable, raging fire, bellowed like a blast furnace, invoking an inextinguishable conflagration, melting steel and glass and concrete, flesh and bone. Bodies instantly incinerated or like rag dolls, tumbled out of windows and fell to their death. It was futility's spontaneous combusted, gigantic funeral pyre. Like sacrificial lambs, they never saw it coming.

Normal people, living normal lives, were blindsided by hell's wrecking ball.

The mushrooming clouds of dust and ash, engulfed, swallowing up the pillars of what had been predictably, routine.

A nuclear blast struck. The gates of hell opened, consuming the infidels and violators and innocents, caught up in the irreversible tidal wave of smoke and flames, a billowing firestorm gobbling up everything in its path.

A diva demolished our physical reality, danced and lapped, torching the material constructs of predictability and normalcy, which offered little resistance, collapsed upon itself, and with a final, horrific gasp, death's arching and bridging across the boundaries and borders, separating the finite world, from the great expanse of oblivion, in its reclamation, bringing with it the dirge of a crackling, hissing, screaming, howling and roaring, ravaging cacophony, for all to be a witness, to an end, imploding into futility.

The pendulum, like a giant wrecking ball, swung into reality's behemoth, a dinosaur whose time had come. Bigger than any other buysaurus, "Skyscraper Rex" pounced on its victims, tearing large chunks of cash out of the competition, armed with the teeth and jaws for corporate predation. These fearsome creatures, formidable competitors in the dinosaur-eat-dinosaur world, were doomed as futility took the reins of a steed that breathed fire and galloped through the canyons and alleyways, corridors and hallways; stampeded through glass and steel; tore down barriers in its full-throttle, unstoppable decimation of time and energy; redefined reality; reinvented the prospect of desolation; and mowed down any resistance to unalterable change.

A killing field like none other smoldered. Ashes and dust choked the life out of everything that breathed a word or uttered a surrealistic syllable of what might be considered, disassembled, existential deconstruction.

The implosion was unavoidable. The house of cards, rekindled the flame by feeding, the unquenchable thirst. The nihilistic beast demanded to be fed. It was the envoy to emptiness, the deliverer of nothingness and the servant of the endless.

Ungohdt/Dohg appeared right in the middle of what had been ground zero. They were bound and determined to make things better, to help heal the gaping wound of a veritable holocaust. They were negotiating with Sea Turtle Nation, an untainted, pristine global wilderness, where all living creatures, big and small were created equal. Their flagship, Sea Turtle Nation gave them the freedom and inalienable rights as citizens of the world and together with the Manhattoes to help them conserve, and at the same time, preserve the natural resources of the island.

Sea Turtle Nation used an advanced sonar system (developed by dolphins and killer whales) to communicate with the Manhattoes. It was a language of the natural world, spoken by those who understood what had to be done to help save the environment.

Xmas Town AKA Spamerica had an insatiable appetite, for accumulating material things. It flaunted its wealth and was showy and gaudy, with a tawdry, incurable habit for junk. The addiction was pervasive. All that was left when Ungohdt/Dohg arrived was known as North

Spamerica, a floating crap game where the final toss of the dice came up snake eyes.

Ungohdt's non was gospel, like scripture, written to invoke change.

Plan-It Kill, an inharmonious dystopia, seen through with one dimensional, rose colored glass out of synch with Sea Turtle Nation, unable to hear the sonar of frequency, used by the denizens of this natural habitat.

A world apart, an insidious, superimposed radioactive gridlock, with a high kill ratio, on a planetary collision course, a cyberspace parallel, out of balance with earth, on a timetable to obliteration, the means to a retrofitted end, disintegrated.

Ungohdt appeared in the image of a humanure. He, of course, immediately declared himself as having no association with any god, especially in the image of man.

Ungohdt was no taller than five feet six inches, with a medium build and silvery, long hair, pulled back in a ponytail. His beard was short and well groomed. His voice had a wonderfully rich tone and he had an ageless quality about him.

Dohg, on the other hand, was a pukka an invisible amorphous creature from Celtic folklore and myth that accompanied Ungohdt everywhere. As if he were his alter ego, Dohg could only be seen by and heard by Ungohdt. They playfully jousted and parried one another as the dialogue, between a visible Ungohdt and an invisible Dohg, gave new meaning to madness.

The non-trees echoed with their banter.

Besides rainfall and sunshine, non-trees used "stellar synthesis" (star power) to grow as opposed to photosynthesis. It was a remarkable source of energy. Within months, Ungohdt's non trees grew upward at an astonishing rate, like a Jack in the beanstalk fairytale, reaching heights of twenty five hundred feet and astonishing diameters. They could be seen by satellites in space.

Ground zero had turned into a veritable rainforest. His poem, "non," was sung and chanted by The Masseuses of Avalon, who resided, in the non-rainforest

and were there to serve Ungohdt and his sidekick, Dohg.

Ungohdt, had a way of being self-effacing and self-deprecating when talking about his poetry. "Who the hell's going to understand this poem?" he would ask. "I know the Manhattoes will. Where am I going with this? They hired me to fight for their rights. This eminent domain thing, that the government is pulling, doesn't apply to them.

"This is their land." Ungodht postured, facing eastward, and pondered. "My staff fashioned from the branch of a non-tree is my scepter. It serves as my divining rod. It helps me ask the question. It helps me meditate. From sublime questioner, inquiry streams. Borne from the non I was probably the first to meander my way through the tortuous channels of rebirth." In repose, Ungohdt closed his eyes as though listening to the prevailing winds.

"How me, or why me, is a mystery," He said. "That humble beginning was not a manger, but rather wrought from the bough of a petrified, non-tree. Gazing into fascination, I awoke. An inaudible, first breath, expanded. And amazement chimed in. Was I the miracle of miracles? Was it a supposition? Or was it a proposal? Was it a marriage of non and play? Was I the question, how or why? 'Now' became my cradle, rocked by non and play. You could say I was parented by

both. Curiosity rambled through me, leaving its mark. Surprisingly, it was a question mark. Love—was it love that had spelled itself out, surrounded by serenity? Was this infinite quietness, peace? What was I imagining? That spark, somehow kindled the flame. An imagination broadened. And deepened the crown jewel with faceted doorways and polished windows, seeing, opening and closing, sealed vacuums and unsealed destinies configured.

“An unnamed organizer structured. A breaker, between rip tides and shoals calmed the estuary as budding newness sloughed off what seemed lifeless began to undulate. Did it move? Was there a sound?”

Ungohdt’s chorus of questions invoked his own answer.

“On its own, a textured, undefined moment, called upon to play—to play sound, to play sight, to invoke the great provider—to change, bathed in the non-of non.

“It doesn’t make any sense. Why keep writing into non-existence, trying to make something out of nothing?”

Ungohdt paused. He was in deep contemplation.

“Maybe I’m experiencing some kind of writer’s block. I’m your classic existential accident, repelling off a jagged, very steep cliff to prove that absolute absurdness is my forte. Sometimes I think I have a very rare form of an inferiority complex. I don’t live up to their expectations. Or maybe this is even a rarer case of inertia. A slowdown is just part of the so-called creative process. Maybe it works in reverse: what slows down is speeding up and vice versa. Maybe it’s just my karma? Or is that being over simplistic?

“I use karma as sort of a Darwinian way to determine what, where, how and when. It's the proverbial scorecard. Dharma plays. Karmic DNA unravels like spools of thread. The needle is threaded. Who and or what fits the profile? Brewing and stewing, from the good, the bad and the ugly, but beautiful in its most pristine nihilistic state, quivers in the morning sunlight in homage to nothingness, is the only way to go." He paused as though composing his thoughts and noticed that Dohg had arrived during his monologue.

"And then there is you Dohg, sort of my Siamese twin. How in nons name did you get here? It never ceases to amaze me. Maybe you sprung from one of my ribs—that is, if I have ribs. "By the way, who invited you to the party? You and that contentious bone of yours that you bury and then exhume, you have a habit of digging it up and then gnawing on it. At least you have great instincts.

"You are my backward half. I have no tendency with one exception: you, Dohg." Ungohdt chuckled to himself, awaiting Dohg's response.

Dogh looked questioningly at Ungohdt. "Why backwards?" he asked. "Just maybe I'm your forward half? Let's get holistic now. Our wholeness is our strength. Ungohdt, why are you trying to be above it all? What does it matter anyway? Who cares? Look—the direction we're going is incidental. The only thing that matters is that we're together. According to gospel I'm supposed to be your best friend, so just accept me for what I am, and in return, I'll put up with your idiosyncrasies and eccentricities." Dohg, an amorphous pukka, changed into a six foot tall, purple

striped rabbit, walking upright.

"Instead of me being your hindquarter lets you and I be the headquarters of what's happening. That's simple, don't you think? Look, there are all kinds of gods in the world just like there are all kinds of dogs in the world. You have more worshipers and I probably have more lovers."

Ungohdt furrowed his brow and angrily replied, "Who the hell are you, my invisibleness? I know, I'll call you Harvey and I'll try to improvise a Jimmy Stewart drawl.

More lovers are you for real!? What does a butt-smelling creature like you know about love? Anyway, according to the humanures that worship me, I am all about love." He signals Dohg, giving him the timeout sign suggesting that they had to take a break or for whatever nonsensical reason, dancing around a non-tree.

"Maybe I have to get a sex change? This anthropomorphic crap is killing me! Of course I'm kidding. That kind of subspecies is something I don't have a lot of time for." Ungohdt took a deep breath and stretched. His antagonist, Dohg seemed nonplussed, unperturbed and unmoved by Ungohdt's gesticulating.

Dohg replied, "I take umbrage at the things you say about me. Smelling butts, as you so crassly put it, is about identifying someone's gender, habits, where they hang out, their diet, whether they take baths on a regular basis.

"Look, in a way, I'm your alter ego, the part of you that's more down to earth. This creator image of yours has got to go. Hanging on crosses and martyrdom is old hat, cliché. Why live in the past? And those books, they keep writing old and new, based on hearsay and second hand information."

Dohg reconfigured into an oversized bloodhound and then into a peacock, showing off his plumage. Anyway the truth is finally out," Dohg said. "It wasn't Jesus Christ who was crucified. It was actually Judas who took the rap for Jesus. All his disciples cooked the books. They falsified the information, and using Judas as a body double, they were able to fool the authorities. The Romans arrested the wrong man. Racial profiling was also around in those days. All Jews looked the same to them. So they shackled and eventually crucified the wrong man. Meanwhile, Jesus was whisked away and escaped with his family, crossing the subcontinent into what is now Turkey and finally ending up in what is now Russia, where he lived out the remainder of his life in total obscurity. "Of course, they had to remove the body from the cave—there was no resurrection—and bury him in an unmarked grave."

Ungohdt:

He looks aghast. He couldn't believe what he was hearing.

"Dohg, that's way too controversial!

I know he wasn't my son.

I do not, I repeat, I do not do the anthropomorphic thing. There is no man or women in my image.

Let me make that perfectly clear.

I do have a very special relationship with Mother Earth. Gaia as she is

referred to is omnipresent.

She speaks with a ravens tongue.

She grows skyward as a giant redwood tree.

She wanders like a great river,

she is a verdant forest and a mountain peak. It's like her franchise.

I gave it to her and she is doing a beautiful job.

Although she is having problems,

with the devolving of humanures, maybe they'll get their act together."

He seems to be weighing what he just said,

while Dohg looks dumbfounded.

Dohg:

Shocked by Ungohdt's statement, Dohg, jumps up and shouts,

"You gave it to her! Are you some kind of power hungry ego maniac or what?!

Maybe just maybe she evolved on her own? She has that innate ability.

She is the consummate artist, her art living through her. What a spectacularly creative, wondrous, irrepressible force!

I wish your Spamerica, run by your humanures, would finally morph into something else more in balance with nature."

Dohg turns his back on Ungohdt and starts to walk away.

Ungohdt:

He quickly walks in front of Dohg, so he can be face to face, eye to eye,

"You have these god fearing candy coated norms,

going nuts. You just can't pull the rug out from under them. You really dropped the bomb this time.

Even though it's true, no one is going to believe you.

The whole foundation of that culture rests on martyrdom.

Whoa, what a blow to the psyche.

Scripture, turned out to be a training manual,

for WMR (Weapons of Mass Religiosity), a nuclear pummeling, good book, thumping machine,

got nixed by an unvarnished,

irrefutable truths or maybe consider a common place truism?"

Ungohdt lost in thought, continued to stare at Dohg, who is starting to look more and more like a Gnu.

Dohg:

Grunting and chanting his mutterings, he ruminates.

"You're talking out of both sides of your mouth. You are supposed to be god

and yet all this ambiguous prognosticating is being expounded by you. Let's get the story straight for once.

Your underworld is a high flying, retro interpretation,

of what they see as heaven

Is that supposed to be your crib?

You and Dante, are reminiscing about,

your toasty little escapades of overcooked prose?

You're like those puffy, huffy egomaniac celebs,

with their garish, haughty, flashy, splashy junk. Overblown bottom feeders, are at the top of the heap of humanures; them and junk, like flies on shit. Stinking up Plan-It Kill,

lower than sewer rats, why do they even breathe?"

He paws the ground and snorts

as though he is going to charge.

"Cha-ching, bling, the nauseating footsteps,

direct from the hood, from Hellywood to Whad Street, cyber pimped knuckle heads. Yes they disgust me!

More dead than alive, it's all relative.

Anyway here we are. You have taken me to what had been a implausible. safe house,

where the average 98.6 degrees, steered their way, to the linear world of norms, carrying out the biz of the day.

And then one day, just like any other day,

it came to an abrupt halt.

The aftermath hung in the air like a shroud or a pall, the haunting, ad hoc, burial grounds, which had without warning, turning into unspeakable carnage."

Ungohdt:

He puts his hand on his hips as Dohg stamps the ground,

"We're standing here, right here, at ground zero,

I'm all about miracles and you're pissing on my extremity. What's that all about? I have to give them hope.

That's why they hired me. That's my job description."

He shrugs his shoulders and at the same time assumes,

the asana of non as he breathes from his diaphragm.

Dohg:

"I don't believe what I'm hearing,

quadruped and a millipede like diamond back, impersonating a bipedal 'purpose', purpose is a one dimensional,

two legged, binary systematic rote repeater; yes no, no yes, right wrong, wrong right, black white,

white and black, upstanding boring pedestrian .

This is getting to be like, a remake of Dinner with Andre or a rerun of The Big Chill. Dining on the leftovers of what's been and gone, rehashed and regurgitated, Ad-Nauseum, dilettante's absurdly posture and pose as imposters." Chameleon, Dohg changes his stance and strut's his stuff, reconfiguring, he once again becomes a six foot tall rabbit, but this time he is colored chartreuse.

Ungohdt:

"You're totally not getting the picture. I don't sit at a dinner table with a Dohg, the arc typical canine or an oversized puka, pooping his way to stardom.

This is not a café in France where they allow pets such as you into a restaurant. I think something is getting lost in the translation." Squatting down, he takes a handful of dirt and sifts it through his fingers. At the same time he picks up a hollowed out root of a non-tree.

Dohg:

He poops rabbit pellets, at the base of a non-tree, while Ungohdt, picks up a shovel and shovels mulch over his droppings.

"Now you're getting insulting. I am as much a part of you as you are a part of me!

We speak the same language.

Nothingness is our voice, emptiness is our ear.

How do you call me a pet? A pukka is not a pet.

I'm a deity in my own right.

And I have just as much right to be here as you."

Yelling, at the top of his lungs, alas only Ungohdt can hear the pukka, who in frustration starts to leap frog across their geraniums.

Ungohdt:

He covers his ears and shakes his head. "Are you trying to be clever? I have this whole universal master plan thing,

worked out and then you come along,

wagging your tale telegraphing some sort of

"I'm happy to see you" message or you're flapping your ears as though unsure and insecure.

Are you trying to tell me something? Is your proboscis, your rudder, to stabilize the whole shebang?

or is it a compass to determine, what direction we are going?

Barking out orders?

Are you trying to usurp, my supreme power?

Or is it, your inimitable way of communicating? Do you run with the pack or stand alone?

A Dohg does not plan. You just live for the moment."

Ungohdt:

"This is not like a cartoon episode of cat-dog,

where the head wags the god.

I am not your posterior.

Let's be clear here, I am your superior.

And getting back to my universal master plan, it's a blueprint on how the pieces of the puzzle,

fit together, harmoniously.

Then I get you, turning the whole thing, into a pissing contest. What's with the accidental and absurd

and your improvised analogy?

Is that what you think of my master plan, just an enormous pile of dog shit,

likening to that sink hole, black hole, anti-matter, swallowed up, so far- fetched fatalistic alchemy,

mixing the absurd, with the accident,

to come up with what?"

He pauses, looking directly at Dohg, seemingly transfixed as though impatiently awaiting some kind of a reply from his nemesis.

"Are you questioning my authority?

Are you trying to subvert my power?

Is this your way of causing, what appears to be, a tug of war?

I'm supposed to be,

the provider of peace and love and you're pulling me,

in a whole other direction."

Infighting, between Ungohdt and Dohg,

colored with futility, basks in the effervescent,

unexpected chance, springing into action

illuminating probability.

The coming out, becomes self-realized. "By the way, who gave you license to do that?

If you try to think outside the box,

you may jeopardize the entire project."

Dohg:

He sits on his haunches and gestures.

"You punish those who doubt you

and go off on some ego trip,

because you believe you're god and those pathetic followers, follow you like sheep.

I'm here to set the record straight.

You bought into that whole, "I'm god" thing and as a result, lost your way.

And the books, those poor miserable dummies, cling to for dear life, can't see the forest, for the trees.

You're the pied piper

and your flocking flock of wingless gooses,

have lost their sense of humor and are weighed down, by the dead weight, of dead serious."

He has an easel setup in an open area, with a blackboard shaped canvas. He takes his brushes and palette and starts painting and drawing a whale and at the same time writes a poem:

A whale's breach
the earth's revolution,
an elbows bend,
and in that crook,
a cradle rocks,
dream time wonder,
a soul unlocks,
guardian angel of the music box.

"The gravity of their gravitas,
is too much poop and not enough spice.
Another words these humanures are impacted.
Nothings worse, than a constipated mind
and an overly strained heart, working overtime, on overload, another words,
a steaming pile of shit, classified,
reclassified and indexed, a referential stack of junk,

stuck in reverse, while straining, for a peek a boo look,

at a future, that doesn't even exist.

A tepid zits bath,

trying to help reduce the swollen,

itchy hemorrhoids of being in the

'now', gets to be painfully honest.

Aching and throbbing, the bulging grape like cluster, of incalculable discomfort, is a head to butt,

major, disinformation highway blockage.

An over wound time bomb,

with a short fuse, overloaded to explode, a dried up, tied up, bound up, locked in the crapper humanure, saddled with a perfunctory purpose,

the workhorses of mediocrity.

The bleeding smart club,

got way too attached to their stuff and when they smart, they really smart (hemorrhoids of course),

looking like sulci of a brain.

Sitting on them, is a painful reminder,

where most humanures brains are."

Ungohdt:

He walks around the twelve acre perimeter of ground zero, sort of surveying the property.

"Look, let's get it straight, I have you on a short leash not the other way around. And I do not, I repeat, I do not, have to be lectured to, by a Dohg of all things. A straggly mutt, who thinks he knows more than Ungohdt. I shall extricate myself, from my hind quarters and somehow disown myself, from a mongrel, which claims to be my conscience and dares to tell me about my ego.

And stop being so critical of my subspecies, the humanares, I have them in rehab as we speak. You may think it's a hopeless cause, but I can see the light, at the end of the tunnel." He stops to and peers into what may be what he is visualizing.

Dohg:

Leaps up, onto an earthen mound and exclaims,

"Are you forgetting that we are attached? I bark you yap. Our thudding hearts, rub up against the same, cavernous wall. Our all seeing eye, sees all, but knows nothing.

And that mindless mind without your conventional thought processes, listens.

Let's face it Ungohdt,

we are listeners and seers,

where it goes from here, your guess is as good as mine. If I am some lowly creature, what are you?

Get your head out of the clouds. Let's get earthy! You go off, on these high wire acts of yours

and tend to fall from grace, after losing your balance."

Ungohdt:

With grand gestures, waving his arms in a circular motion, he beckons,

"Look Dohg, I came here originally to help rebuild these twin towers that

were symbolic of T-Rump capitalism, the generically branding ad infinitum. Mediocrities branding iron, redundantly rubber stamping from one "Crap Slash and Be-gone", on and on and on! Nauseating, to say the least!

And now they will be twin totems, to a proud people, the Manhattoe. We must restore their dignity. It's their land and we must bring back an unspoken reverence for all living things, robed in a spirit world, for posterity.

The twin towers, which crumbled and turned to dust, right here, right on this very spot, must not be restored to their glory days." He turns on his heels, "I mean towering edifices, destroyed by a pending finality, which has haunted civilization since recorded time. The existential rebirth of futility rears up unannounced and consumes our skyscraper oracles, to unavoidable descent into the interminable.

We have no choice the indigenous people must be recognized and acknowledged as Nature's guardians and caretakers."

He looks toward Dohg as though looking for his input. He holds up his CD that he recently released, filled with songs that have an edgy, political satirical message.

"I repeat I want to get the ball rolling. I can't have another civilization, just vanish and disappear."

Dohg:

Both look at each other. The silence is deafening and then

Dohg breathes diaphragmatically and assumes the asana of a yogic master.

"With all due respect, are you crazy? Beside the debacle, rubble, ashes and dust, they left a paper trail, leading into the backroom slugfest of, "who's got a deal?"

Deal makers, shysters, hucksters and shylock,

and these nine to fivers,

stuffed into what would turn into a snake eyed deathtrap. "The Casino Futile" that day, at that moment,

had the chips fall and the Collector was there, to cash in, those I.O.U's. And all that paper tallied up, zeroed out.

The weight of futility, encased in glass and concrete, collapsed. Like printing presses,

knocking out towering edifices,

like giant billboards summarily demolished.

Cardboard artifacts, of a faltering, dying culture,

nickel and diming it to death, the imponderable dam of hidden cost, shook violently, right down to its foundation, the floodgates swung open, the forces of the unexpected, broke the bank.

Coming in, over budget,

the lumbering behemoths of commerce,

living on painkiller pay dirt,

drilled for fool's gold,

in cubicles and cramped office spaces, cyber spaced humanures, rolling the dice, in an air tight alibi of ultimate inevitability, just a mouse click away,

from self-termination.

'The Spamerica Oligarchy, The Xmas Town cadre of

was in the cross hairs of the great annihilator.

Vlad "The Impaler", procreator slammed into the body of evidentiary obsolescence.

A spark as futile as creation itself ignited a firestorm.

A macrocosm, in full big bang regalia, ceased to exist.

The unending saga of beginnings and ends, filled the imperceptible void of nothingness,

a vacuum where atmospheric pressure, dissolved and the oxygen was sucked out,

of an intangible prognostication.

It went the way, all big shebang's go,

the absolute ultimate 86ed. "The grease paint and saw dust, were swept away and before you know it,

there'll be a new circus in town."

He takes another deep breath and continues his unscripted rant,

"A fragile, top heavy payload, disintegrated.

The bomb was dropped.

The tip of Manhattan became a 2001 Nagasaki.

Errorists inside and outside the glass house,

were headed for an unavoidable collision course."

A clash of cultures exploded. Belief systems warred. Terror stricken errorists, erred.

Fear and distrust spearheaded the attack.

One had planned it, the exact date and time. The others never saw it coming. Opposites attract!

The meteoric shock wave,

gave new meaning to a meltdown.

Primordial elements were responsible for the invocation.

Fire danced, against the skyline.

Air fueled its diva. Water and wood played too.

The children of a new dawn

were just on the other side of a distant horizon.

But first the playing field had to be leveled.

Deconstruction, razed the fallacies of heaven

and delivered on the ground zero,

inferno of hell, blinded by festering complacency

and a deaf ear, deafened by the mashing roar of apathy, accessing a motherboard,

to crash and burn, on the disassembling highway.

Buysauruses, like giant limbless,

subterranean beasts, jutted upward,

towering monoliths, gobbling up the sky,

occupied by denizens writing themselves off, unknowingly reporting,

on an unpredictable doomsday trajectory,

that already had come

and gone leaving its indelible mark.

Posterity, would never know posterity,

because there would be no posterity.

Delusional self-absorbers, were demolishing one thing and at the same time, reconstructing,

a virtual reality, hostile takeover.

A parallel universe hovered. The illusion swirled. Seemingly indestructible,

the jutting monuments to power and greed, were suddenly iced. The Titanic "Tower of Power", a BS-2 replication, a floating crap game on the Jersey shore, went belly up. "Crooked" FYI King Con AKA Blabber T-Rump's crapshoot's bankrupt five times, a 950 million dollar Taj, smashed into the jagged edged iceberg (filled with creditors he screwed), an invisible futility floated in a vacuum filled with the vagaries of nothingness.

It was hell's coming out party, in all its infamous glory. Rivets were ripped out the hull. The failsafe system failed.

The vessel that was unsinkable,
suddenly was struck by a mutable force and sunk,
into the conflagration of change.
Built to withstand any unforeseen danger,
the bulletproof exterior exploded and shattered.
The confetti for parading civilization,

paraded into the hollow vastness of ubiquitous emptiness. Another words it had to happen. There was no choice.

The firestorm ignited. The deadwood went up in smoke. The new growth had already rooted itself in the anabolic resurgence of timed destiny.

"A preeminent beginning,

rode in on the coattails of self-imposing finality".

He paused and gathered himself.

"And after all that, you're now telling me,

"the natives are restless"! Are you nuts?

Red man versus white honky! No match. Game over.

The white guys (specifically El Presidente "Crooked Don" T-Rump), are claiming, eminent domain. They aren't about to give up, this super prime piece of real estate, to the help, those enslaved by corporate terrorism, the big biz steam roller, rolling over the natives, leaving in their wake, a take no prisoners, slash and burn policy."

He cocked a leg and relieved himself.

"The humanures drove themselves to that precipice and then jumped, not by choice, not planned and totally unpredictable, termination was in the mix and there was no way to stop it."

The perilous unseen reared up.

The past was obliterated,

falling backwards in time,

exposing the underbelly of what drove them, to an unavoidable conclusion. A house of cards, collapsed on itself.

The shocking truth, about dissolution,

is that you never see it coming.

And if you do, you try to stall

for time against the rising tide of the inevitable.

A silly smile, flashed across his face as he closed his eyes and his armadillo body started flashing like a strobe light.

Ungohdt:

If looks could kill, Dohg would really be in trouble. And then he broke into raucous laughter. He didn't believe what he was seeing.

"Why you four legged, hydrant pissing upstart. What do you know about anything? You love that Dohg profile Humanure's best friend! You're just an amorphous intrusion, into my privacy and tranquility.

Those that died in some way or another believed in me. Are you going to make it a wrong place, wrong time equation? What are you some kind of canine philosopher, who thinks he knows, what caused the rise and fall of the walled in empire?

Granted I had some influence, on the way they were doing things, but I didn't tell them, to overkill the thrill of the ride, I mean ride the wave like your surfing at Malibu, and whatever you do don't get greedy, so what do they do, they get paganism on me. Worshiping me, god, in their image is blasphemous. Idolatry in the form of towering glaring cash cows was their choice. They didn't consult me. And this salvation thing, on their part, is such a cop out. I mean, own up, to the monstrous mousetraps you have built."

Steel girders melted, under the heat.

Reality was suddenly, without warning, torched.

The inferno was like an enormous fire sale.

Everything must go.

The creaking and moaning and groaning conjured up. Bodies in free fall splashed down.

A Cashier cashed in, the chips.

The pizza girl and the water cooler gang,

were silenced forever.

Tragedy struck and the death knell rang unstoppably.

Sirens screamed. How do you measure a holocaust?

Is it by the number of victims?

Rescuers triaged and sacrificed.

"Hey listen Dohg, I do not want to get into some tiresome, blame game, with you. They bungled the whole operation. It became a compartmentalized, massage parlor, figuratively speaking, you pat me on my back and I'll massage your purpose. You know, that linear mind game, locked into, an anal retentive, exclusionary clause."

Corporate hubris,

with that lumbering, bumbling swagger,

turned into the hostile takeover. "What was I to do? Errorists flawed by imperfection, failed to listen.

Thinking that they were perfectly right, errorists erred.

You do not know who or what they were? "

Dohg looked at him in, disbelief. Now in the form of a Panda Bear, he gnawed on the stalks of Cannabis bamboo shoots, which grew wild in this non rainforest.

"You pretend like you have all the answers, but when push comes to shove, you give me this look of exasperation and bewilderment. Like you haven't a clue what I am talking about?

I represent most importantly the Manhattoe's and all living creatures big and small."

He crosses his arm and purses his lips as if he were defending his position.

Dohg:

He sidled up to his companion and sidekick and begged the question,

"What is going on with you? And who the hell are Errorists? An anticlimactic constipated crowd is your creation? We are in serious trouble, if that's the best you can do.

Or maybe it's a persecution complex, whatever it is you've got me scratching behind my ear not because I have an itch, but rather,

you leave me asking the same question, is god terribly lost or what?"

His Panda Bear colors changed from,

black and white to red and yellow.

Ungohdt:

He pointed, took his forefinger and placed it on his right temple and amusingly smiles,

"Don't get smart with me.

Errorists are those that are right minded norms,

which binge on liquored up good books,

glassy eyed drunkards, quoting chapter and verse, intoxicated with the spiritual value of a fart in the wind, looking for a desktop,

short cut to charbroiled heaven,

but are walking terrorized terrorists,

terrorizing themselves to death,

with reason and purpose sticking to the script, they live by a book of rules.

One is a passive terrorist,

otherwise known as desk sitters,

in the company of those, whose terror is buried in,

the walled in set of values, a system of squared off mediocrity; too normal, too safe.

The other is a zealot terrorist, blinded by a manufactured hatemongering, skewered and impaled by conviction,

they were about to end up as overcooked kebobs, eaten by rape artist virgin bitches, twenty four to be exact."

Dohg:

Shaking his head in a sort of questioning manner, he laughed and then cries tears that fall like snowflakes.

"Now you are really infuriating me. Why attack bitches? I have met some really hot bitches in my day.

Oh, I see, errorists are walking talking mistakes,

which think, they are always right,

because they are going by the book, when in fact they're malignantly, painfully wrong and so,

they automatically kill what's painfully wrong.

That's going by the book.

So the pain in the back or your neck

or your chest or wherever, is isolated,

targeted and then killed.

Armed painkillers,

armies of them, with an arsenal of weapons and drugs, kill, "kill or be killed", microbes, kill or be killed terrorists, kill or be killed, just for the sake of killing.

If it's in the bible, a bible of divisiveness and intolerance, prejudiced by what they believe, their fundamentalism, is hell frozen over, so they are always skating on thin ice, frozen in time, painkilling, killing in the name of their god, drugged with linear purpose.

Straight jacketed humans degrade. They then incrementally and sequentially, devolved into humanures.

Now I get how it works.

It's become a world full of terrorists, terrorizing themselves, fearing fear itself and the fearsome wrath of self-denial,

in an all-consuming, internal battleground.

Scourging and flagellating and flailing and being skinned alive, self-loathing and abhorring, “whose that in the mirror”, a war zone keeps warring, jockeying for position, exhausted, burnt out,

at a dead standstill, nothing changes as the erring errorists, think they got it right,

having erred, on the side of right,

they lopsidedly dysfunction.

That level of constipation isn’t even on the map.

They are off the score card.

But from apathy to atrocity, complacency to flagrant denial,

they live by their good book and they’ll die,

by their good book.

Creatures of habit, consumed by assuming,

that those that don’t believe the way they believe, are bad, evil as the opiate of hate is mainlined.”

He digs around the base of a non-tree, giant roots are exposed and he starts gnawing on them.

Ungohdt:

He shook his head, threw his arms up as if exasperated.

"Dohg, you're way too judgmental. Errorists, are the core group of the subspecies, known as humanures. That moment of impact, when jet fueled flying WMR (Weapons of Mass Religiosity), slammed into the macrocosm of what was to become, a doomsday apocalypse.

Gang banging believers,

flying straight into purgatory,

on a junket to the immovable brick wall, to them it was going to be a paradise,

instead it turned into garbage,

garbage thrown into an incinerator,

like the one, in a ghetto apartment building, incinerated with the rest of the garbage, spending death as fundamentalists, barbecued char.

And these bozos put a god, their god front and center? It had nothing to do with me. Anyway what god in their right mind is going to allow druggies, drugged on Madras, brainwashing

and bible thumping mind control,

chapter and verse junkies, to slam into a building, strapped to a deathtrap, wrapped in the pages of a so called good book, no one has the right to do that,

that's subhuman, inhuman and degrading and degenerative, and so,

here's where the devolution of humanures began.

They are byproducts of a morphed hybrid, unfeeling, unemotional blinded by hate and vengeance,

ending up as scattered ashes, like overcooked dog shit.

Linear, one dimensional errand boys,

crazy glued to a diabolical purpose,

decided to take, a sightseeing tour of hell

and ended up staying, for an indefinite period of time.

Humanures are cut from the same,

whitewashed cookie cutter normal and safe generic criteria. Strung out on busy, busying themselves to death,

the homogeneous serial killer, kills for the sake of killing, a lascivious habit, that "needs to do more", redundant, repetitively, validating killing, becomes the drug of choice.

Predictable, planned,

a calendar of wants and needs,

overbooked and overworked, becomes a major stressor. And it all fits under the one category, belief.

A structured, inflexible rigid, stiff, uneasy, roller coaster ride, with lots of peaks and valleys,

worn out, so very tired, restless, victims victimized, by second hand facts, hand me downs,

shop worn and inaccurate, misinformed, spoon fed with pabulum disinformation,

on a cyclonic demolition derby. A real twister!

They are junk store junkies, cooking their self-absorbed, textbook fact based pile, into very believable bullshit.

What a load! Every pore reeks,

from the worst smelling crap, anyone has ever smelled

and that's mediocrity.

It's this dank, dark milieu, in a cesspool of complacency and apathy."

He knelt down as he sipped tea from a large saucer. The tea was from very large flowers, growing in his garden, which resembled chamomile. He boiled the water and then let it steep for about ten minutes. It was very fragrant and had the full bodied flavor like red roses in bloom.

Dohg:

Crouched down ready to expound, Dohg, looked at Ungohdt in puzzlement.

"Do yourself a favor, lighten up. What a horrible guilt trip. Hey, look at it this way, they are what they are. Locked into gridlock, is what they think they want and need. They built their own proverbial mousetrap, so let go and let Dohg. Yeah, that's right. They need to listen to me more and not so much to you, Ungohdt. You're not nearly as important as you think you are. Anyway they misquote you and turn the whole truth thing, on its head. How can you know truth, when you don't even know who you are? Talk about a gruesome, grotesquely genetically engineered.

they pull up their shorts, so high up their crotch ends up, in their brain. Butt hole brain, is a tough act to follow. It's like their blow hole. The worst case of an anal retentive head trip, slips into a comatose, no-brainer. They are wedging themselves, into hell and damnation, all the while calling it heaven," (Hellywood)

jumped all over this one, on the back lot of tinsel town alley).

"And why bullshit,

it doesn't have enough nitrogen.

It's got to be chicken shit. And that's how they live it,

chicken shit replicas, redundantly hardwired, to the privy of their insatiable greed, beady eyed Blabber T-Rump (FYI "Crooked Don", MLPD Multiple Liar's Personality Disorder shuck and jive impersonation of Rudy Kazoo, his mouthpiece shylock, talking out of both sides of his mouth, wearing the fact checking common sense lies of Captain Underpants)

They're up to their eyeballs in T-Rump's Swamp. A toxic shit hole painted white on the outside. An ivory tower sitting on T-Rump's Swamp quicksand sewerage filled quagmire, overflowing with T-Rump's brand, "Farce and Fluff", "big mock" chow. The feeding frenzy, money-whore greenback, junk pigging out. Bloodsucking leeches. Hosed down, exposing CMS-666, an army of suited up clowns in a "Cirque de Farce", D. C. (Douche bag Cons) circus applauding BS-2 nativism, misogyny, racism and the 3 C's (Collusion, Corruption, Conspiracy), sinking into a paleontologists wet dream. Digging up dirt up from BS-2 Hubris, the fossilized ammonia dyed hairdo singed and buried under the rubble of a self-subscribed nuclear holocaust. BS-2 a peeving, petty unlike Hamlet, unwashed blood on his hand, prisoner of his whitewashed slammer, sodomizes his bestial urges. His self-propagated, "The Witch Hunt" broomstick prima facie evidence that he's not making it all up, while surreptitiously shafting his rabid mob, while trying to sweep his junk under the poisoned well of both shithouses, Con-Us, CMS-666 (Constitutional Muggers Scumbags).

An epoch where before bullshit was recognized as "bullshit", BS-2 was supreme ruler, whose oval shaped orifice, in between gluts, normalizing asinine sandwiched in between plastic, T.A.R.P.'s (Troubled Assets Relief Program), CDO's (Collateralized Debt Obligation), swaps, flips and flops, they became hybrid derivatives, victims victimized by their own demons, like the Krells, in that campy movie, "Forbidden Planet".

Here's where we got, "truth is stranger than fiction", and they're living on what now has become Plan-It Kill, those humanures, consumed by the monster, from the id! A B movie, horror show, is how they're living it. And all Hellywood can do, is keep on cranking out, its own autobiographical star studded, fart imitating fart schlock. That's what happens when you try to ingest too much celluloid. The end result is gas and lots of it.

These strutting, over-dressed cleaned and plucked turkeys, walking the red carpet, a mob of sycophantic fagots,

gobbling their way, to the glitzy whorehouses, lined with glamour pusses, who adulate and compromise themselves, fleshpots under the spotlight, bipedal vermin,

looking for more attention, than they could ever deserve."

Ungohdt:

Unhesitatingly responds, flinging a rock, he picked up from the ground into the air.

"Dohg, Dohg take it easy. Just go with the flow. It sounds like you're writing their obituary. They don't know better. Matter of fact it's all they know. It's like a knee jerk reflex.

"Maybe Pavlov would have something to say about it.

I have other things to tend to right now.

Go see a play if you're bored.

Join the theater crowd. Broadway's gismos and gimmicks are a concocted flimflam, upstaging *Cats Got The Runs* and

Aquarius On Life Support, or better yet,

Vlad the Impaler and Crooked Don "Go Viral"

a morbidly obese BS-2 egomaniacal "fat cat",

a comic book, goldbrick, garish tower, overpriced, staged, indulgent, shit hole commode.

What a weak-kneed pisser!
Dohg, go get a ticket and make sure
to take your vomit bag with you.

I have a project to complete.

Right now the road map is our blueprint to this societal devolution.

Revolution implies change and they are not ready for that. Evolution stopped about two thousand years ago,

when the unintelligent design crew came on board and Iscariot was fed to the "walking feds", feeding on gangrenous dead meat.

I know one thing there will be no skyscraper here. This is hallowed ground. That's why you and I, Dohg, are disguised as a vagabond and his Dohg/Pukka—and you stay invisible, for obvious reasons.

In this politically correct world, they now categorize you and me as homeless. That's part of their dehumanized, desensitized mind fuck. Dignity doesn't enter into their equation.

Whatever happened to the noble vagabond?
Socrates' offspring, questioning and searching
for the truth and for Diogenes' torch,

which brought light to what was hidden in the shadows so that we could see beyond petty differences?"

Dohg replied, "Too much information. Who the hell's going to read, this scrawling, bile-filled, global gall bladder of yours? This bilious, livid, counterfeit globe, with three quarters of it shit canned, under water?

"Even what was once known Iceland, was broke. The frozen tundra of Bank of Spamerica is trolling for taxpayer dollars, smelling like sardines stuffed into a can of I.O.U's.

Smelly mother fuckers,

doused in jet fuel and bourbon, propped up on chairs, pleading their case, to the lowest form of life

on Plan-It Kill. The legislative body, 'Con-us,' is in league with their cross-examined bedfellows. Miscreant consumptives,

swallowing the cum of the mug shot. Jerk-offs, spitting cobras, slithered into a C-Span camera's eye,

scaly suits and ties, the thin skinned vipers, trying to look like Cheshire Cats;

questioners perched, pompous jackasses strung out, power-mongering junkies, stinking up the joint

like snake oil salesmen selling "Too Big To Fail," believing in their own bottled hogwash.

Sniveling and whining with forked tongues, tasting and testing, soothsayers,

spitting out venomous words, blinding and inveigling, they show their true colors.

Impotently grasping for straws,

cold-blooded sycophants, poison the well. Deviants banking on stealing the hearts and minds of those that trusted them derail"

"Dohg," Ungodht interrupted. "Back off and slow down. Take a deep breath and smell the roses. Look, it's a balmy night here at the southern tip of lower Manhattan. What could be better than springtime in New York City? Just get a whiff of those ocean breezes, Dohg. Maybe it'll lower your blood pressure and you'll

be able to calm down.

"Just on the other side of the Hudson River is Mexiraq. And to the north is Canadastan. And just up Broadway is Whad Street.

You know it's a parallel juxtaposed virtual reality, Wall Street's fast track,

six furlong dog and pony show,

where the dog ate the Ponzi scheme and the pony grazed on the Hedge fund.

The wadded-up Wall Street got its gonads ripped out

of its socket, so a bunch of pussy whipped Madeoffs sucker punched the suckers. The ham hocked,

greediest of the greedy took them to the cleaners. I mean cleaned them out, so that the naked guy, walking around with only a barrel to cover him, becomes the poster boy

for Calving Clone's billboard on Times Square, showing off Bernie's cash draw, inflated junk,

trumped by Goldman's ball sack, a simulated sow ear, filled with raw sewage.

"Do you know what it's like to sit bare ass on a whole bunch of goose eggs? They're doing a reality show about it as we speak, called, 'Rhoids Gone Wild.'

"Oh, on Whad Street there are wads and wads of wads, the tin cup gonads, serving as a collection cup.

The cups are always half empty as the hand out becomes the recidivist behavior of Freudian frauds,

who slip into the deviant behavior of screwing the public doggy style."

Ungodly laughed hysterically. He finally calmed down and turned to his pukka.

"Dohg I am not referring to you, so don't take it personally. I respect you. This is purely an allegorical way of demonstrating how low these lowly creatures have sunk. As a matter of fact, they had to foreclose Wall Street (Whad St. is a parallel universe, separate and distinct from Wall Street, a virtual reality, mimicking the economic downturn, somewhat dilapidated and rundown). All that property is being auctioned off at bargain basement prices.

He goes into his dwelling, followed by Dohg, lights a candle, made from the sap of the non-tree and then takes his manuscript off the bookshelf and starts thumbing through the pages.

"And now, let's get to it. The book is going to be something like a narrative."

He began to chronicle events and storyboard his script.

"What the hell are you narrating?" Dohg asked. "You and I are camped out at the bottom of Manhattan, with barely enough food and water, and you think because you think you're god, everyone is going to stop what they are doing just to listen to you? Are you forgetting that when you're disguised as a vagabond with a straggly pukka, it's not like they're about to get us an appointment with the Pope or Oblaba? They don't even know who we are. As a matter of fact, they think you're off your rocker. We know who we are, but unfortunately they do not have a clue.

"You never heard of Oblaba?" Ungohdt looked at Dohg questioningly.

"He's from the mouthpiece offices of Bushwhack & Oblaba. Bushwhack was voted in as the black card president (the ace of spades president, a dead-on, arrogant honky, a green-horn spelunker in the Tora Bora Mountains, looking for bearded boogey men, as he goes AWOL in a seven-minute petite mal seizure in a classroom full of second graders. Oblaba is the white knight, the white card president, riding in on a dead white horse. The rest of the cards are your stereotypical bad guys, including Sodomy Whozinsane).

The dunce doodling dummy
who spells cat with a K;
he was the leader of the 'fat cat pack;'
he's the Alfred E. Neumann,
the poster child of the 'What? Me worry?' of Mad Comics.

"You claim to be god and you never heard of Bushwhack? He subbed as the blackjack dealer in the oval office.

"He just launched his IPO Terrorizeme Inc. It's a new board game called 'Waropoly.' What were once countries became Waropoly properties that the player buys up by first invading and then by warring, and then by occupying, and finally by displacing its citizenry.

By monopolizing he made a killing.

Then he went to the 'Too Big to Fail' card,

dealt from the bottom of the deck.

It's kind of like a form of nepotism,

the inbreeding of cock suckers, sucking up to each other, sucking Benjamin's loins posthumously. It's pretty sick.

But they are a pretty sick bunch of old guys.

They are called old guys

because they spend a lot of time together,

jerking each other off, double dealing and squealing, and of course stealing from whoever they can steal from.

They talk double speak, in order to cloud the issue.

They're ramping up, 'dumbing it down,'

and all the while, in true errorist fashion, they think they're smarting it up.

Greed and power has its own self-serving language. Its part of the Waropoly

credo: 'You get to keep what you steal.'

Of course it's about killing, duh!

Are you that dense, god? Pay attention!

Now they are actually in the research and development stage of a high-def video game called 'Waropoly.' Mainstreaming killing is a major part of his marketing strategy. Bushwhack is lobbying to get it a G—Nonviolent—rating.

Con-us is now in session voting on that earmark.

It's part of a bill they are trying to steam-roll through. It'll pass faster than you can say bullshit.

'Get your prostate whacked and radiated.'

'Get your hearts ripped out of your chest, we got the valve job for you.'

That's how they're advertising and promoting sick care as "hellthcare". And tacked onto their sick-care as hellthcare bill is none other than Waropoly.

Bushwhack, is just riding, the gravy train wave, into hijacked killing.

He's about to cash in. And his pals in Con-Us are on board too."

Ungohdt, took a deep breath, assumed the posture of repose and shook his head incredulously.

“Now you are really getting crazy on me,” he said. “I got to get more protein in your diet. Bushwhack? No, I do not know a lot about him, other than the fact that he has a ventriloquist as his second-in-command, Beelzebub Feigny uses “old wooden head” (an endearing nickname for Bushwhack) as he affectionately referred to his president.

“Teleprompters are out of the question, since Bushwhack has a problem. He is monosyllabic, so they don’t want to confuse him.

“Oh yes, and let me not forget his not-so-secret weapon, Rover Ambush—his pudgy, alter-ego-cum-bastard, his hired back stabber. Ambush ran Bushwhacks campaign like Goebbels: go for the jugular and takes no prisoners. They made quite a couple, Bushwhack and Ambush, in the right wing of the Right House.

Dohg shook his head, from side to side and danced around in circles.

“Too much information, I’m in contact with Barney, Bushwhacks canine, telepathically, and he gave me the inside scoop on his purple dinosaur impersonation. Barney is an overstuffed, ball-less T.V. Rex, busing his scrubbed and polished little retrofitted goodie two shoes, to the safe and normal junk in the box depot of pussies gone sissy, in the emasculation of the Spamerican kid.

"And Oblaba is a reverse Oreo cookie,

lily white on the outside and black as coal on the inside.

It's all part of the blah and blasé culture. The human race got aced out by the devolution, turning into a perfunctory binary system; devolved Humanure.

"An oxymoron superlative,

lie and cheat and call it truth, half-truths are good enough. Whatever it takes

to get ahead veers sharply

to being right, when in all truth, it is wrong. Find your own examples. They are out there. It's a cultural phenomenon.

A double barrel shot gun:

one barrel shoots faster, the other needs more buckshot, gridlocked, locked and loaded into two fisted, white-knuckled distresses.

And then the pile-on is triggered. Old habits, like old tapes, keep playing the same recycled platitudes, Déj□ vu is the old news becoming old tapes playing, 'here we go loopy loop;' the broken record reruns of 'Ground Hog Day.'

Caught in a virtual reality tread mill,

they spin their wheels. The meter is running, they're out of time and they're frantically gunning it, looking for a killing."

Animatedly showing his playful side, his mane swooshed.

Ungohdt climbed up a non-tree and sat on a branch, munching on a non seed.

"Enough! You're being too critical.

I wish I was back in non and I didn't have to be exposed to humanures' descent into mediocrity.

When they had their humanity,

they had so much more promise.

Too bad they cannot get past their utter devolving into unalterable junk, into rapaciously accumulating crap, and then labeling it global warming or greenhouse gases, cancer, diabetes or developing an institution like Violentology to make violence, cult. "You don't get that fucked up through osmosis.

If lockup is a rattrap and their spoon feeding you

the gruel of subconscious wanton killing, then you kill what you feel, kill what you think,

kill the dream, kill the magic; and then they rebuild you from the ground floor up with a sub mock-up of who you are supposed to be. Your former self has been torn down and destroyed.

"That's a gun to your head. That's passive aggressive violence, shutting down an original and turning into a reasonable facsimile a carbon copy is where humanures have gone." He turned toward the garden and walked along a pathway in the company of his pukka.

Dohg scampered and darted between trees in his own inimitable way.

"Ungohdt isn't that what you're doing? Tearing it down and then rebuilding it?

"Are you also a cult? Where are you going with this? You have quite literally

an army of addictive painkillers. You're demonizing what they were originally

and then comes along your typical rape artist preacher, teacher, dangling the proverbial carrot (which is actually a bone of contention, and if anyone should know about bones, it's me), promising them, figuratively speaking,

a pot of gold at the end of the rainbow.

And there you are, as circumstance has it:

you're sitting on 'the pot,' stuck between a subconscious urge to kill and a passive aggressive ambition to kiss the ass that cons you into a depressed, suppressed and of course repressed, murderous, supplanted rage. You're now the surrogate mother fucker, blinded by Lianetics. Downing huge quantities of cloyed hyperbole and chunks of heaved ego crap, the breakfast of chumps. It has you humping the El Don Hubbub mannequin, ruler of Mexiraq and author of Lianetics.

I know that sounds somewhat convoluted,
but I'm a Dohg and this is how Dohg,
a mythical Pukka, expresses himself.

But getting back to the pot, you didn't shit, so the backup ends up between your ears and there you are, a shit-for-brains victim, reciting other people's shit. Is that stupid or what?

"And then to the north you have Elvis Judas Krist as the new president elect of Canadastan. He was a one-hit wonder. Yeah, he used to be in the music business. They called him 'The Phantom of Pop.' Don't you remember his album, *SHAM IN THE MIRROR*? He reinvented himself. He started a whole new career in politics. And now he's running a country." Dohg slapped his flank with a paw while at the same time scratching his head and reciting a pukka limerick so softly that Ungohdt couldn't hear it.

Ungohdt perked up, trying to hear what Dohg was saying, while laughing to himself. "You're like a living, breathing newsroom, a gossip columnist all wrapped up in one little Dohg. You must be the reincarnation of Hedda Hopper. I mean, you got it down to a science. You must be the only one in Spamerica who has his finger on the pulse of what's going on in the world, especially because you're a Dohg. How many dogs can claim to be a walking talking newsreel?"

Dohg snapped back with a half snarl and a half guffaw.

"Sarcasm doesn't suit you. I am just trying to fill you in. No skin off my nose if you're not current on who's who. "Lianetics is the book that spells out humanure devolution. And its author, El Don Hubbub, visited his taxidermist not that long ago. Yeah, he's been gutted and stuffed with voluminous copies of his Lianetics books. His message and his stuffed, waxy cadaverous will live on posthumously." Dohg laughed like a hyena and

ran in circles. "I don't know what the hubbub is about?" asked Ungohdt.

"Violentology, as far as I know, has sold millions of copies of Lianetics.

According to Violentology, it's important that you live the lie but cover it up with subliminal violence, with crow bar effectiveness, pummeling who and what, you thought you originally were, to death, with a sledge hammer meter meting out punishment, with the punisher breaking you into fragments and then reconstructing you

as a babbling tower of Lianetics.

El Don Hubbub cloned replicas, robotics, reciting chapter and verse." As he talked, Ungohdt whittled away at his hollowed-out non root. He was fashioning a musical instrument, using a diamond-shaped leaf from a non-tree as a reed for the mouthpiece. He blew through it, producing a drone sound somewhere between a

didgeridoo and an oboe.

Dohg watched and listened attentively. He seemed mystified by the sound of Ungohdt's instrument.

"Whoa, that's too heavy," Dohg said. "You're dropping a bombshell. I don't think they're ready for it. I know what you're saying. Violentology is like a skin flick, except you leave your clothes on while you get fucked. And talk about skin—humanures bare it all!

That's it, they are only skin deep. Skimmers, barely scratching the surface,

one size fits all, caged cunts and dicks, UFTs (Ultimate Fucker Tricks), skinny dipping in high gloss on the cover of *Crotch & Tits*, a magazine loaded with 38-caliber, naked shell casings, empty and desperate for attention, they porn themselves at a level of violence under the radar, selling their asses to the lowest bidder, repackaged and resold;

children of the dammed, pawned and enslaved, pimping media and absentee parents; self-absorbed, preoccupied tabloid sensationalism is grist for the mill; souls are lost, hearts are killed and lives are permanently maimed and destroyed."

Tears welled up in Dohg's eyes.

Ungohdt walked to Dohg and put his arm around his pukka.

"It's the fornication invasion!" Ungohdt exploded.

"Fuck you, fuck me, fuck them, fuck each other,

it's a fucking war zone, orgy of fucking killing. Kill what you feel. Kill sex. Kill passion. Kill love. There is no love! Only fuckers, fucking each other

a fucking match to the death.

Promiscuity is just another word for fucking,

kids fucking kids, color blind killers, taking the truth, their innocence and what is honest and fucking it to death, until the dream of what was once their inviolate innocence is killed."

Dohg pulled himself together, trying to compose himself. He grabbed hold of Ungohdt's shawl, woven from the Cannabis bamboo stalks. Dohg kept pulling on the woven strips of the cotton-like fabric.

"Ungohdt, Ungohdt, slow down." Dohg pleaded. "You're scaring me. I love your passion and what you have to say, but you have to make what you're saying a little more palatable.

I hate to go off on another tangent, especially at this deeply poignant moment, but those non seeds we've been eating have miraculously been helping me. I've never been so regular. It has to be roughage at its best, especially for my digestive system.

And the garden that you started just a few months ago is turning into a

forest! I had no idea that those non seeds had that kind of growing power!"

Dohg picked an apple-sized radish out of the garden and started to eat it.

Ungohdt grabs a succulent non fruit, which looked like a cross between a mango and a banana, and took a bite.

"Yes, the non-seeds just have to be planted in the ground and they grow like wildfire. They are somewhat like plants and trees that grow by photosynthesis, using oxygen and carbon dioxide and the light. Well, my non seeds use stellar-synthesis, drawing from what humanures call the universe,

all the star power, anti-matter, and positrons, and they miraculously convert greenhouses gases to pure oxygen as well as replenish the ozone layer. This could be a whole new way to create jobs through alternative anti-energy called non-fuel, far more effective than any bio fuel.

We're starting off as a cottage industry.

It's just you and me, Dohg. We're the original, a DIY (Do It Yourself) phenomenon.

"What was going to be a garden is turning into a rainforest and an amazing vegetable garden. Who would have guessed? Even I can be surprised, sometimes.'‘

"But Ungohdt, come on!" Dohg said. "They are trying to throw us off this land. They don't care whether you're god or Santa Claus. It doesn't matter to them. They filed the papers in superior court and they just served us. They have the National Guard right outside our front door. The feds are the main culprits. They won't leave us alone. El Presidente "Crooked Don" T-Rump and his henchman are claiming eminent domain and are trying to take away, what rightfully belongs to the native people." He hid behind the tree to peek at the artillery pointing in their direction. He spotted a sniper on a rooftop and ducked for cover.

"They have us surrounded with tanks and everything else they have in their arsenal to throw at us. They are ready to take us down. Are you sure it's okay? I know you think you're immortal Ungohdt, but we got a real problem here. They are doing everything to criminalize what's going on here. I think it's beautiful, but they are really threatened by it and the humanures are living in terror.

"I know you are all about tackling 'crisis,' which means growing and changing, but I don't know if they can handle it. A healer to them is an anathema."

Ungohdt looked unperturbed as he stood in the direct line of fire, almost daring them to shoot.

"Dohg, cool it!" he said. "Have faith. Those warmongers are spineless. While on the other hand, our trees stand for freedom. That in itself is magnificent. These are majestic sentinels, guarding the natural world, pristine and untouched!

"Protectors of our environment, each one a beacon light, a towering colossus, with branches, like the arms of Atlas holding up the sky. Trunks are ten meters in diameter." He walked inside the enormous, cavernous base of a non-tree, where he and Dohg resided. The interior was a rose-colored, sparsely furnished, cedar scented dwelling. The earthen floor was cushioned with forest mulch and the ceiling was like a church steeple. Ungohdt peered upward through what looked like a great spire. He then walked outside and continued addressing the issue at hand to Dohg.

"Non-tree whorls hold the secret to the ages." He embellished, to prove a point.

"Being in the moment empowers us, like having guardian angels shielding us from the deleterious effects of mercurial toxicity. And this is our forest of arboreal splendor.

"We are to be caretakers, preserving its sanctity. Normally I'm not into angels, but at this time,

at this moment, I accept them as providers and protectors.

We will go to court to fight for our rights and our freedoms.

I will not let them desecrate this holy ground. These trees, originally from the non, are already a thousand feet tall.

They will grow rapidly, given the climate, eventually reaching a half-mile high; and that will happen probably within the next six months. When they reach that height, we will be able to mine from their roots gold, jade and silver, in their purist form; and as an alchemist healer,

I will bring to this besieged world, with the help of these precious elements, a

panacea."

He bent down and began digging under the mulch, where the non-roots were.

Dohg pooped a large pile of dung-like manure right at the base of the tree as he continued to dialogue.

"Don't get carried away. Your humanures are into the medikill disease model and you're going to talk to them about a magic potent or a healing amulet? You're going to tell them about trees that are five times bigger than six blue whales, that contain the life force of ten universes and also telepathically with the reverent forests of this world?

These trees are holistic sentinels, standing guard.

Your humanures are out of sync.

They're not holistic (even those who may think they are). Here's the forest and they can't even see the trees (I admit, the analogy is getting a little old)!

Once again, 'it's the blind leading the blind.'

As soon as they can get through so-called legal channels, once they get the okay—and most likely they will—

you watch, they'll come in here with bulldozers and wrecking balls and explosives

and turn your rainforest into splinters and pulp." Ungohdt raised his fist in defiance and then saluted his trees, the guardians of his sacrosanct.

"You're asking them to think outside the box and quite honestly, they really don't know how," Dohg continued.

"I think what you are trying to do is a gallant and noble cause, but who's really listening?

Humanures lost those listening skills generations ago. Everything is weighed and measured through a referential, politically correct world. Whatever they think they know goes through their filtering system. Their oxygen-starved brain's becomes ischemic; they shrink and quite literally wear out (just take the fact that 26 million people have Alzheimer).

Theirs is no spark to rekindle the flame, and the most important system of the body, the 'breathing system,' shuts down. "They have exhausted their resources and are running on fumes. It's why SCA (Sudden Cardiac Arrests) kill

so many humanures every year

(about 1 million a year die from SCA, with a 5% survival rate). First, there is not enough oxygen for the heart to function, due to a malfunctioning breathing system; and most importantly, humanures are emotionally shutdown and spiritually bankrupt (if you tell them this of course they'll deny it). They're all on life support, sleep walking, arthritic, stiff and rigid and inflexible, in a semi-comatose state of apathy and complacency, being entertained by the most crass, unholy garbage:

"Gooey gaga junkie
Entertaining biped, war-hogs, jam,
hogging the junk in the box,
channeling boobs,
strapped to a 42nd Street, throwback freak show, cartooning circus clowns
with gaga goo, goo unoriginal pop ups.
Pimped and pilfered,
the pumped up audience
gets to be part of a double blind study
on BS-2, Swamp King,
micro-televising, through an existential backchannel,
over exaggerated, overexposed his lens is in front of a visceral camera,

shooting his delusional cold hearted cruelty. It becomes a backdrop to the depths of

his depravity emasculated personification,

Magnitsky is impaled by Vlad the Impaler,

His corpse, beaten and battered, is dragged before Con-Us MS-666 (Motherfuckers of Shit) and what appeared as an act punishing oligarch's, sanctioning them, freezing bank accounts,

BS-2 broadcasts live in a self-absorbed filming of a tortured soul, lashing out

At innocence, perverting truth, so his power can corrupt his tawdry cheapened

Disinformation and misinformation, gold plated tinny retribution, purposely hurting those who are weaker and poorer and disadvantaged. His motive is simple.

"Me and Vlad are pals. The D. C. (Derelict Capons) mob is invisible holographic images. Bot trolling, hijack. Executioner, Vlad the Impaler, executes Anna for reporting the truth. He manhandles El Presidente "Crooked Don" T-Rump. Hells stinky shadowy figure, shows the world how brute force rules. "Crooked Don" is impressed. Called a dotard by a murderous dictator, he takes center stage with a bitter enemy, shakes his hand and tells him how smart he is. MLPD (Multiple Liar's Personality Disorder) face-off, pretense and disingenuous, eyes insidiously driven by the same demonic evilness, shake hands. They are standing on the world stage, demonstrating the same sociopathic, egomaniacal urges. Reality show barker, fires "the enemy of the people", encourages violence, blasting his way into the limelight, flooding the airwaves, taking down the firewalls to protect and defends, he does the indefensible, colludes, misuses, and conspires for only one name, one brand, without truth, without loyalty, without honor or dignity, a modern day Benedict Arnold, sells out to a malicious adversary. BS-2, The Grand Wizard of QQ (Queer Quacked) carded, rally around, "The Fuhrer of Oz".

Clubbing them to death with a branding iron,

Tiger's woody got stuck in the wrong hole. All I can say is that it wasn't pretty.

His roar turned into a whimper. And the media got plastered and blitzed it.

His million dollar trophy got blonder
as she kicked his ass all the way to the bank.

He showed his girly pussy side. A toothless, clawless predator, dining on white meat, got to be an overexposed, philandering gobbler, a rape artist.

His coming out party was quite a bash,
with truckloads of cash and a flurry of sponsors,
flash flood alerts, drowning him in tabloids.
Paparazzi tiger tamers
with whips and flashers got his attention.

They are the bottom feeders,
feeding on their own kind;
ladder climbers, clawers and rippers,
armed with insatiable ambition,
stock footage, showy stoppers,
in the all-seeing eye of public domain,
are fed to the jagged toothed
minnows sitting in living rooms,
vicariously stuffing their faces
with jail bait porn,
killing and overkilling the same images,
in a bloodless bloodbath
of hemorrhaging glitz and flesh-eating glamour.
Pusses strung out on wanton greed.
plant themselves in front of the camera,
ravenous for attention,

it brings out the killer in them.
Intoxicated with the killer drug,
fame, it gets shoved into vanity's mainlined disdain.
Destitute, coiffed and couture,
craven creatures prey on
adulation and narcissistic pandering.
The bunny hop, suicidal,
follows the pied piper joker
and they go batty as they sign
on the dotted line,
agreeing to a contractual death sentence.
Splashed across the front page,
the catwalk, fleshpots, prostitute themselves.
Sleepless in Hellywood
is an old movie,
telling and retelling the same story.
Under each star
on Hellywood Boulevard
are the washed-up,
buried bodies of those
that didn't make it;
the nameless, faceless, forgotten,
who dreamed of becoming someone famous;
unfortunately, they got to see

the infamous side of the coin."

Ungohdt finally responded. "Drama, drama what a pile of perfumed dog shit, Dohg. You amaze me! Where did you get all this information? Are you

spending all your time reading those trashy rags? Did you typecast them? Are you judging them unfairly? Are you reading this from a script? Maybe you're smarter than I thought you were? Your observations are very astute.

"Of course it's an uphill battle.

What can I say? I'm on a crusade.

Those aerobic cherry pickers are eating up the publicity in their one-dimensional straightjackets.

the fastest lane slammer—and don't forget to throw away the key.

The hotter the studio gets, the faster the melt down. As they all smell a rat, playing the same old tune,

'Rat Race,' in a hell-bent lock and load; Hellywood's stylized fucking machine,

segued into the I-Yank-Wanger practice of a self-indulger, cadaverous corpse posed.

Jarhead Bucksheimer is mass producing

nickel and dime shows like a jack off rabbit, celluloid bunnies shot on location,

bipedal props on overkill, with slick, glossy shellac veneers and smooth liquored up, varnished dialogue. Scripted thespians,

in a lifespan of a thirty minute time frame, using carbon dating forensics

to determine the end in record time.

"Hey, Dohg stop pissing on my trees!"

"Why? You said we should pee and poop around the trees."

"That's true," Ungohdt said. "Since we're eating fresh, organic fruits and vegetables from my garden, and our waste is higher in nitrates, it makes for very

high quality fertilizer. Look at this mulch on the forest floor, it's like a beautiful, rich carpet, you could almost eat it.

"And our composting has paid off. We are finally starting to see the fruits of our labor, Dohg."

seaturtlenation@gmail.com

The kihl thrill ride:

North Spamerica is the world comprised of the

U. $. A. (Unholey $tate of Apathy) and Canadastan to the north, sharing a 1,234 kilometer border. To the east of the U.$.A. is Mexiraq, sharing a 743 kilometer border. Mexiraq traffics huge quantities—thousands of kilos—of a chalky powder called Kihl. A corporate raiding party downsizes. A hostile takeover is in the works. Drug lords in the border towns of Mexiraq dispense massive doses of Kihl. Kihl is a synthesized drug, made from the mutated Kihl fungus, grown on the high plains of Mexiraq. The genetically engineered Kihl, was first developed in Spamerica by

Trumpscum Inc. The project was classified. The government kept it as a top secret project. It's grown in underground hothouses under ultraviolet lights 24/7. It's gray and greenish in color and grows profusely, emitting a musky fragrance on jet-black coal tar derivatives.

A large, portly man sits behind a very ornate impressively mahogany desk. He looks pensively at something he has written; he seems intensely preoccupied and then addresses board.

"The company that got the no bid contract did the research and came up with a synthetic formula, but they….I mean it does what it's supposed to do—that is, what it is designed to do—that is, it simulates virulent parasites, bacteria and viruses. It's a pathological pathogen, a stimulant, overworking, overusing and infecting the brain, so it starts to breakdown those targeted areas of the brain that require sleep. It depletes oxygen intake, causing serious restlessness and sleep deprivation. It blocks dreaming and shuts down independent thought and an impassioned sense of freedom. That's all killed by taking kihl. The heart rate variability (HRV) is significantly, but subtly, altered. Chaotic beats, counterpoint, play into a harmonious tempo, which insidiously becomes dissonant, causing a dis-eased (distressed and uneasy) signal that interrupts normal function, and so the natural rhythm of the heart is compromised."

This is the latest memo from Brass Ballufux, CEO of Chemosatanics, Inc., a major player in the manufacturing and distribution of Kihl. He also has the secret formula for his corporation's worldwide drink, Koke. He knows all about branding and Koke is the drink everyone is drinking. Koke has eight teaspoons of kihl in each bottle. His plant does the manufacturing and bottling and is very involved with the marketing and distribution of Koke. Ballufax is also a major player in corporate U.$.A. He is the bastard illegitimate brother of "Crooked Don" T-Rump of Spamerica. Very well connected, he has met with, solicited and retained the services of Bushwhack and Ambush. He is the chief executive operative for Spamerica. Playing ball with all the big wigs for his self-serving purposes, cold blooded and ruthless, he micromanages his empire with an iron fist.

Machiavellian to a fault, he could be the carbon copy of the Marquis de Sade. His bestial, insatiable ambition has turned him into a monstrous sociopath. For example, he was breeding a new type of grotesquely engineered, freakish beast called the hogena (a cross between a gigantic wart hog and a hyena, the fiercest of predators). He had been commissioned by the Spamerican military to genetically design such a 'animal', by splicing DNA from a animal who had contracted Apathy Infected Dis-ease Syndrome (AIDS) with the chromosomal DNA of wild animals. From that splice, a genome was manufactured that could be duplicated and cloned, with the capability of reproduction in the laboratory. Apathy of the animal would morph into ferocity with high enough dosages of kihl.

A sterile killer was born from the Frankenstein like experiments of Brass Ballufuxes Corporation. Bred for use in the battlefield, the hogena was designed as a super predator. But unbeknownst to even President Oblaba, these beasts would be

unleashed for the very first time, by the military at the tip of Manhattan, at ground zero, where the non-forest grows. Ungohdt and Dohg would be their first guinea pigs, so to speak, in a vile evil act.

Brass Ballufax is ready to launch his controlled, apocalyptic, money-making operation.

Ballufux reports to his board members at a meeting in a garish, ostentatious downtown skyscraper, owned by "Crooked Don" T-Rump, and his kid Clone T-Rump. Daddies bad-boy, "Love it!", the dirt on his most disliked, possibly hated femme fatale, in an Oedipus throwback to his wet nursing, living in pop's "Twisted Mangled", game show image.

"The good news," he tells them, "is that all of this is under the radar. Our kihl ratio is so high that it is most definitely producing the desired results: chemically blocking dopamine and serotonin and shutting down the pineal gland, so our target market is sleepless, restless, and obsessive compulsive disordered. We're on the fast track.

Tension levels soar.

Stress degrades.

Self-absorbed and preoccupied,

the virtual reality treadmill kicks in; rat racers abuse and misuse.

Habits become incurable addictions. Gorging on want and need, staying pathologically busy,

the morbidity of that frenetic pace keeps them obsessed with time-crunching deadlines,

blind to see, too deaf to hear, mission accomplished.

Our consumer fits perfectly into the disease model. Ratchet up the drudge factor and we'll make a killing." Ballufux finishes his speech and then looks glaringly at his board. There is a moment of silence and then they burst into applause.

The credo of walled-in Wall Street: pirate formulations, steal intellectual property, and permit fraudulent activities of a high stakes, take-no-prisoners, go-for-the-jugular enterprise. Boarded up, the heart of Spamerica is collapsing, but the backroom wrangling—wheeling and dealing—goes on, like a runaway freight train; a train wreck in the making, plays the big board like Russian Roulette, in a remake

of *Apocalypse BS-2*. It's a rerun or a replay in their backyard. Guns to the head, locked and loaded, just another roll of the dice determines who will be the lucky one to savage and rape First Lady Medusa, mannequin trolled by

Neutered Kinkbitch, BS-2's QQ rapacious loquacious verbosity gone foxy, newsy ham hock propaganda machine in a revved up spin cycle, brings down the "House of Barbs", a white Claus Barbie pressure cooker replica, crematorium like atmosphere, where nobody is anybody's best friend, the scuttlebutt, water cooler tribalism of outright backstabbing and betrayal. All orchestrated by El Presidente "Crooked Don" T-Rump.

El Don Hubbub shoots up his own Lianetic, super-size-me junk, ingesting high doses of Kihl. He and the violentology cartel are looking to buy out any competitors. "Get me more. I need more Kihl!" Hubbub exclaims. There's never enough. "Look at those stupid Spamericans, they crave it. They are our best customers. It gets them crazy, which is to our advantage. I am about to go to a summit meeting with Elvis Judas Krist and President Oblaba. Kihl is the first thing on my agenda. The FDA (Federal Drudge Association) should approve Kihl. Its like melamine: it has many applications. You add it to baby formula, add it to a drink, use it as a condiment.

"I have the report right here from Brass Ballufux. According to him, all the studies have shown that kihl does what its supposed to do, that is, it over-stimulates, gets the consumer revved up;

gets the brain overworked

so that it short circuits in those targeted areas. Decreased oxygen intake damages the neurons.

"The imagining nucleus is destroyed. All of that, according to his scientists, is repressed, suppressed.

The release valve for hormones and enzymes is shut off, causing

our potential customer to have an urge for more kihl.

We now have it as a preservative

in all the vaccines, which we manufacture, right here, in Mexiraq.

There are seventy-five side effects, listed in the fine print

that our consumer doesn't bother reading."

Hubbub points to the graphics and barely legible label that appears on each and every bottle of his products.

He continues, in a nearly strident tone.

"The immune systems are blown out. Autism in children (in adults it's called dementia) has increased tremendously within the last twenty years, as well as diabetes and arthritis.

We are constantly opening new markets for our products. We also control the generics and OTC (Over The Counter) drugs. We are constantly expanding our market share. And the good news is that all of this is under the radar. Get this—kihl acts like the number one stress fighterby ramping up the stress levels. That works in our favor.

Depression is on the rise amongst old and young alike, as high levels of drudge go undetected. We back the medikill disease model.

That's our bread and butter.

In this economy, the disease industry is recession proof. We promote the pathology; that's not even in the medikill textbooks yet. That's how new this stuff is.

We have our end users, clamoring for more junk.

Tension levels soar. Multiple stressors (environmental, chemical, over exercised, over use, exhaustion) attack the breathing system.

At the same time, we are able to decode the CNS (Central Nervous System). Dendrites wither. Synapses are clogged and blocked with drudge. Self-absorbed and preoccupied, humanures devolve; the virtual reality treadmill kicks in as rat racers abuse and misuse.

Habits become incurable addictions.

Gorging on want and need,

getting so busy that our customers punch in, but never can punch out as the clock keeps running, the tank is empty, and the energy dissipates. So our targeted consumer, whether on the battlefield or in the aisle at War-Mart, become potential killers, strung out on copious amounts of kihl.

But we do have a problem,

which I have discussed at length with Brass Ballufux. This joker calling himself 'Ungohdt.'"

El Don Hubbub sinisterly chuckles.

"He and his so-called sidekick Dohg, who is his constant companion—a puka—can you believe that!!?—have been like a thorn in our side, trying to blow the whistle on us. They must have a mole, an insider, filling them in, on our activities. It's baffling. We have the best security in North Spamerica. How could he possibly know what we're doing?

Anyway, they keep putting out a newsletter and press releases, trying to expose us to the media.

We don't want that kind of publicity. We are somehow going to have to take care of the problem. He's become the voice of the Manhattoes.

"I thought we got rid of Injuns a long time ago. The natives, my ass! We poisoned their waterholes, got them boozing and binging on kihl. We decimated their population as planned and still they want back what they claim is theirs, our island, the most valuable piece of real estate in all of North Spamerica! We have to wipe them out. Eradication has to be our final solution. But this Ungohdt character has taken up their cause and is bringing way too much media attention to what he calls their 'unalienable rights,' according to the constitution.

"What civil rights is he talking about? Habeas Corpus is a thing of the past. Forget the fourteenth amendment and all that due process crap. We have to take these bastards down and out." He pounds the desk furiously. Turning beet red, he stammers and then continues his ranting.

"And then he's been pushing that holistic garbage. I thought our marketing campaign, I.S.I.S. (Idiot Squad for Interbred Savagery), would override all that proselytizing nonsense.

"He's saying he's the messenger. He's not god. I hate to be the bearer of bad news, but his savior kick doesn't have legs.

"Humanures don't have time to listen to that. Anyway, they have hellth insurance, which is really based on a sickness model, and those that are not insured still have access to our product, so they, too, will be consuming large quantities kihl.

For now, no one's buying into his holier than thou crap. It's the fact that he perseveres that's disconcerting. He doesn't let up. Someday, someone is going to take him seriously, so that's why we have to end it now. We must be discreet. It has to look like an accident."

The backroom of El Don Hubbub's presidential mansion is filled with a smoky haze, from kihl being smoked and snorted by members of his staff. Mixed with tobacco, the unmistakable, acrid smell of kihl hangs in the air. His henchmen don't say a word when El Don Hubbub is speaking; after all, he is the author Lianetics.

As I speak, they're trying to pass a hellthcare bill in Spamerica. It's being debated on the floor of both houses. I've had my lobbyists hard at work promoting kihl, and because of kihl, we can get on board with the medikill profession in promoting degenerative disease. That's where the mega bucks are. And to make sure it's a slam dunk, I've retained two very important big shots: Bushwhack and Ambush. You can't go any higher. Bushwhacks got his Waropoly war game as an earmark, upgraded as a militarized version, and my weapons-grade kihl is attached to his earmark. How can we miss?"

WHAD ST.

Meanwhile, Ungohdt and Dohg are carrying bundles of fresh organic vegetables and fruits, as well as necklaces, made from non-tree seeds, as big as large marbles. They took the non-seeds from the sweet, succulent fruit of the non-tree—fruit that, opalescent in color and reflecting light like a prism, looks like precious stones.

Ungohdt and Dohg go out through a trapdoor in their dwelling, a secret passageway, it appears to lead to an underground grotto with a narrow corridor under a waterfall, cascading into both a cold and hot spring. In the water and on the banks of this pristine pool are five very beautiful, nymphs of the forest of non, called the Masseuses of Avalon. They are clothed in gorgeous dresses made from the bark of the non-trees. Stunning and absolutely sensual, they serve their avatar, Ungohdt, with utmost devotion and obedience. They cold press fragrant oil, from the seed of the non-tree, which they use for a tantra healing massage. They are able to open the chakra's and chant Ungohdt's mantra GUI-TOL (pronounced GUY-TOL, god union individual total one love), invoking a resonating river of light that at once illuminates and enlightens.

They live for their Ungohdt, in his "House of Disbelief."

Ungohdt and Dohg slip past the guards, making their way to the theater district. Taking a route they have traveled before, setting up shop on the corner of Whad Street and Wall Street. It seems to be symbolic as the two parallel universes intersect. Wall Street was once hub of the global economy. It has now fallen into ruin.

Buildings are abandoned. Running the risk of being found out, inconspicuously as possible, they disguise themselves as street vendors. Ungohdt has brought his guitar with him. Whad Street is suspended in a celluloid, colloidal solution, a floating virtual reality.

The illusion of business as usual is illusory.

The lens of a 16 mm projector

projects a grainy picture on the floor of the stock exchange, like a holographic image.

It's like a silent movie.

There is no sound.

You can see hundreds of shadowy figures, buying and selling, frantically bidding as the hustle and bustle is magnified

in a black and white matted texture. It all seems bigger than life, but in all actuality, there is no life—only a deathly quiet, like in the arena after a fierce battle has been fought.

In a theater that engages in a war,

where in the aftermath, a chilling stillness prevails. Here, in this war zone, there are no winners or losers,

only a deafening silence, scarring the landscape. Crossing the threshold of no return, the age of greed and power has met its demise.

The hollow sound of the past rang like a death knell.

The cries of those who lost their lives, lives cut short, sobbed uncontrollably.

Tragically, ground zero became the site of a mass grave. Frozen in time, this catastrophic event will always be immemorial.

It was Ungohdt's way of immortalizing a time

when only silhouettes, painted a picture of a dying civilization, whose material needs outweighed everything else.

A physical world overstocked with things.

Borrowed time had a very short life span. And the proverbial grindstone,

like a giant eight ball, rolled down Broadway.

The two standing pins were knocked down. It was a strike. The snow ball in hell melted. A fragmented, shattered world reemerged from

the blinding smoke and choking dust.

Wall Street devolved into WHAD STREET.

It was somewhat like the Las Vegas strip in its heyday, where the north end

of the strip

was now old and dilapidated,

like the land of the walking wounded,

while all the latest ersatz, schlock, amusement-park hotels were on the south side. Garish piss pots lashed to I-beams;

glass and concrete palaces of glitz; pantheons built for the sole purpose of inveigling lustful worshipers of cash

crashed and burned.

The unchecked excesses became fuel for an abysmal firestorm.

There was nothing to prop up

what was about to come tumbling down. The overbuilt big houses cracked under pressure. "The sky was falling."

Rag doll bodies, defying gravity like wingless butterflies, fell to their death. Audible thuds of body projectiles

hit like a gavel as a judge passed sentence. The fallacious notion of safe and sound could not circumvent the gate keeper, executed by the masters of futility, whose episodic deliverance came at an unexpected time.

The theater was crowded with those looking for closure.

The play was not on Broadway.

There was no marquis, only those abandoned extras, unscripted, unaware, and ensnared in the unexpected.

How could they know? How could anyone know?

Flames left deep battle scars, pieces of burnt flesh and bone fragments, unrecognizable. But those who were lost, wandering aimlessly,

were unable to find closure. The writhing current had washed away their loved ones.

The rip tide came from a broiling sea of emptiness. What could they salvage from the wreckage? They all took pause. How does the world stop so suddenly?

How do you pick up the pieces and then go on living? How futile to try and avoid the unavoidable.

It must come. It will come.

Hitting against angular cornices, shattering bones, break and fracture, shearing through the pain, a painless free fall lets gravity increase, the velocity of interminable fear, giving way to a fearless acceptance, squashed by an imponderable end; the dismantling, laid bare, the fragments of what was, once whole.

There are no longer hands of a clock.

There are no names, no faces

only the sound of a ticking time bomb.

Where in the universe will it strike next?

How long before tragedy is played out

on the stage of happenstance?

A tragic play runs simultaneously, with millions of other tragic plays

as the comedic jester looks in the mirror and laughs. How many times and places coexist?

Timing is everything. But the unexpected is a fulcrum, bringing truth and balance where confinement and your self-definition suddenly went up in smoke.

Maybe, just maybe, they had been liberated. The physical constraints now were gone and they now had discovered a new found freedom.

Wadded up lives spat through hollow straws, derailed and self-destructed, shedding the debris of the past.

Packages shrunk as the bankroll

turned into a fist full of I.O.U's.

But to get out of the way of the express train wasn't easy. Every thirty minutes, the non-train would come roaring through the center of WHAD STREET. Passengers were seated as well as hanging from straps,

seeming almost motionless.

Faces of despair relived tragedy.

It ran up and down WHAD STREET.

The ghostly whistle stop express tunneled into unstoppable futility, fading, echoed into the abyss of nothingness. Specter riders stared into emptiness,

soulless screamers, howling, peered into the unknown. Engagers, engaging in disengagement, lost in finality;

undisclosed disclosure, slammed shut. Their fate was sealed.

Since their arrival, Ungohdt and Dohg have made a point of getting Ungohdt's message out there. Fearless and self-assured, he sermonizes, genuinely trying to get the humanures' attention, but they are distracted by other things.

Redundant "to do" lists,

an army of the neediest,

hardwired to a needy habit,

strung out on busying,
busy, more need, to do,
hooked on the lethal junk,
freebasing needs, controlled,
shot-up abuse, a rock pile of lost souls
addicted to their addiction,
self-absorbed preoccupied minds.

Ungohdt and his faithful companion Dohg have a natural way of unwinding. Like pied pipers, they are momentarily, able to somehow make their audience snap out of it—out of their drudgery, apathy and complacency. They throw a repose breaker, which turns on the light, regenerating the spark, which rekindles tranquility.

For some reason, the humanures are drawn to them. They don't know exactly why, but they listen and are intrigued by Ungohdt's passion as he lithely performs an almost ritualistic song and dance, "Here are the Keys to the Stage Door." He points to his heart and moves gracefully, turning toward his onlookers as if his audience is a group of courtiers. And when they ask him his name, of course he gives them his alias, "Dr. Summon."

He is the apex healer, from the non and this is the one name, chosen for him to use, when in Spamerica. The crowd laughs incredulously. "Dr. Summon, what could he possibly be doctor of?" Ungohdt, posing as Dr. Summon, tells them that he is a holistic alchemist and he will give them his secret potent, which will serve as a panacea. They do not know what to make of what he is telling them. They question is validity. "Where are his credentials? Why is he here, on Whad Street, pedaling his wares? And singing songs like, "The Doctor is in?" Not exactly a show stopper, but what he calls "Quantum Rock."

He shows them how eclectic his music is, going from political satire to a song about children and then he launches into a song called "Masseuses of Avalon." They absolutely love it. But who are they, the Masseuses of Avalon? He tells them, "In a relatively short period of time, you will know who they are."

How fascinating, he is, to them. If he were Dr. Summon, why would he choose a pukka, Dohg, that no one except him can see, as his only companion? How crazy and absolutely ludicrous! He is always talking to his Dohg as though the pukka understands him. The Dohg is either a figment of his imagination or he's completely off his rocker. Bonkers, is the consensus.

"Where are you going with this, Ungohdt?" Dohg asks. "I hate to be the bearer of not-so-good news, but your playbook is falling on deaf ears. Your efforts to expose the powers that be, are probably those of a quixotic crazy man. Here we are, you and I, on Whad Street. Wall Street, for the most part, is all boarded up. It's turning into a ghost town. And here we are, trying to make a few bucks, while you sing your ridiculous songs. I mean, they have something to say at least, but who is really listening? We are having some luck selling these non-seed necklaces. The organic vegetables, from our garden are selling, granted, so at least we're making enough to live on."

He bends down and puts his face in the squash blossoms, closes his eyes and enjoys the moment. Ungohdt looks at Dohg, with a whimsical smile, on his face.

"Dohg, don't be such a pessimist," he says. "Cynicism is fine, but being as skeptical as you are just gets in the way. The theater crowd loves us. Who knows where it'll go? You can already hear my songs on the internet. 'WHAD STREET' gets the most play-time with its cryptic signature sound and political satirical message. Whad Street has potential.

"By the way, I have spoken to the landlord of that boarded-up theater over

there." He points in the direction of a rundown, art deco building, with a large marquis, wrapped around and hugging the front of the theater. Unlit and with no letters, it seems to be a stark reminder of heydays long gone.

"He has consented to give me nine months, rent-free, if I do all the renovations. Guess what? We are about to open our first Repose Lounge from Ungohdt's House of Disbelief. Come on, let me introduce you, to our future landlord and let me show you, the art deco interior of this theater."

He grabs Dohg playfully by his bushy tail and pulls him in the direction of the theater. "It's really beautiful. I will, of course, bring The Masseuses of Avalon here to perform. They will sing and dance in the legendary mythology of the non. I hinted to them that this is going to be their new home. Words cannot describe their excitement."

Dohg tries to extricate himself from Ungohdt's grip on his tail.

"Ungohdt, you are such an incurable dreamer! Where are you going with this? Wake up and smell the rat poison. You really think, the city, is going to give you a license, to operate a theater? If anyone is delusional, it's you. In the face of the adversity we come up against every day, you're going to take it one quantum leap closer—to what could be curtains, for us. You are now exposing us, in a way, which could be very detrimental to our health. They are going to up the ante. There is no question: they have a contract out on us and it's been signed, sealed and delivered."

"With your kind of optimism, I might as well close up shop and go home," Ungohdt replied. "Dohg, where's your adventurous spirit? We have a chance to save the environment, show that it was the sacred ground of the Manhattoe Indians, and that it must be given back to them.

"I must admit, I finally had the realization that this epoch is defunct. Buysauruses and what they stand for are extinct. We are here at the southernmost end of Manhattan, at ground zero. It makes no sense to rebuild what has outlived its usefulness.

"It's time to restore the pristine beauty on consecrated ground for the virtue of freedom and well-being, liberty and justice for all.

"I hope I don't sound too preachy. That's not my intention. We have to show the humanures how to get back to their roots and their origin. Unfortunately, democracy has been subverted and replaced by marionettes in a staged, overdressed puppet show. It's an Oblaba cakewalk, Harper's Bizarre, law school treatise, on 'shuck and jive'. Flashing his toothy whites, the mouthpiece gets to firebomb the jury, in a torrential snow job on, 'Too Big to Fail.'"

seaturtlenation@gmail.com

U.$.A. (Unholy $tate of Apathy)

Ungohdt prepares his editorial for his monthly newsletter, *Time to UNWIND.* His Masseuses of Avalon distribute it, disguised as mannequins in drag. They literally boggle the imagination. This month's editorial's theme is the Unholy $tate of Apathy. Having completed his lengthy article,

he reads to himself.

"Time to UNWIND: Unholey $tate of Apathy

Even the government is privatized. Take, for example, Spamerica, U.$. A. (Unholy $tate of Apathy). It's all window dressing. Voting has become, like a fixed horse race. We really don't get to vote. It doesn't count anymore. They are no longer elected officials, not really. They are, in all actuality, appointed by special interest groups and lobbyists representing major, terrorist corporations. Global conglomerates, lumbering behemoths hold them hostage, playing the "Too Big to Fail" card.

Mexiraq is just a puppet government of Spamerica. And Bushwhack's Waropoly, is how the U.$.A. plays the game; invade, occupy, privatize. And to the north is Canadastan with its supped up pork bellies, flooding the market, with genetically designed porkers, from stem cells, so they can mimic any organ system. They have the organ eating market, and the genetically engineered organs for transplanting into humanures.

The macabre has become the modus-operandi of the industrial complex of Spamerica. Pork ears, pork hearts, pork genitals, let's face it, pork is the name of the game.

Those rigged pork bellies are loaded with hydrogenated fats, trans fats, the worst of the worst drudge stimulators. Pork bellies have turned into an incredible bonanza for Canadastan and their president, Elvis Judas Krist. He's cornered the market. At the summit meeting next month, Krist, Hubbub and Oblaba are going to make a deal."

In the great rotunda of Rump Towers, Brass Ballufux's booming voice echoes, "I'm getting Krist one million kilos of Kihl and he's going to cut me in on his Canadastan pork bellies." The U.$.A. has become the global fence. Pushers, legislate their own self-serving, hidden agendas are drugged on consuming junk, power and greed. It's becomes a hardwired familial trait. A generational hybrid devolves.

Enemy combatants may be your next door neighbors, so if the profile fits, kill your enemy. If the pain you feel doesn't belong in your life, if there's no time for it, if it's not on the calendar, then score massive doses of painkillers to kill what you feel.

You've branded and labeled your own worst enemy: a punch drunk with power and greed, the poster persona, "Crooked Don" T-Rump..

The diagnosis and the treatment for the terror of pain, the terror of fear, for

the terror of anger, for the terror of what-you-don't-know is to kill, invade, occupy and mask or deaden the symptoms. It runs off the overcooked books of "The Farce of the Fleece", by a blustering, loud mouthed, misogyny's blowhard, none other than, El Presidente "Crooked Don" T-Rump.

It's Medikill's sciences terrorist predation. Kill what you feel. And when you black out from the overdose, you never wake up. The very last symptom you try to kill, sadly, but ironically, is you; an irreversible flat line.

Maskers mask by repressing, by shutting down pain, anger, and fear. Overkill, goes From Columbine to Parkland, the plethora for violence is institutionalized, woven into the fabric of a culture repressed, suppressed, in the medical disease lockbox, oppressed depressant, getting locked away in a prison of unrequited depression. The results: mass murder. That shutdown can be a cancer, a cellular freakish mutation, a molecular time bomb, a messaging-and-delivery system breakdown. A symbiotic meltdown, that produces a fogged, distorted signal, a nuclei army, armed with the osmotic aberration of internal, warring factions.

Balance transmutes into imbalance, devolution, in static disharmony.

That all adds up to, imponderable weight, bearing down, eventually exhausting and depleting.

War plunges us, into a dark, craven quagmire, where evil fogs, the mirror of our souls. A video game raises the stakes. The kill quotient must be met. Troops become pawns. They are merely widgets in a failed experiment.

A sinister wedge issue, sacrificial lambs are led to slaughter, lauded and praiseworthy; they are above reproach.

Like toy soldiers with bulls' eyes on their backs, they blindly march into the meat grinder, pulverized, by the pulp mills, disseminating disinformation, like embedded chips, in the mindset of jingoistic terror.

It's demonic and far from being heroic, when you kill in the name of suited-up terrorism; a justifiable, ravenous, insatiable appetite, for killing. The torture chambered amputees, are walled into conditional response, compounded by a head trauma that sends the wrong signal.

Going back into battle, is like going backward in time, reliving what killed you—or a part of you—in the first place. And when the thrill ride ends, and you have to go back to civilian life, the edge is gone. "Put me back, in the front lines! I want to 'kill or be killed.' My life has hit a plateau and there's nowhere to go. War is my platform, my springboard, to catapult me, into the theater of war, so I can act out my aggression, my repressions, my depressions, my suppression.

War is my drug; I want that high. I want back my hero status. "Give me a gun. I want to be Johnnie, but I don't want my face and limbs blown off, I just want to follow orders, and kill when told to kill, just following orders.

What a rush! I have a weapon. I have been deployed. Now I am confused. Why am I here? Who is the enemy and what do they look like?

I know I got a job to do. And at the end of my tour of duty, how do I sew back my arms and legs? Where do I get a new face

and a new heart and a new soul? At which body shop store, can I buy half a head?

I've got to get back, into combat, with my fellow soldiers and fight, what I was taught was right.

I'm addicted to war and I have this compulsion to kill, but I've been told that's my mission and I'm just following orders."

Gun stores and drug stores draw a parallel, storing potentially, lethal weapons, storing munitions, encased killers, an arsenal, tabulated, prescribed, are designed to kill.

The common thread, tying them all together, is violence. Violence takes many shapes and forms.

A magazine, loaded in the hands of a violator, has become his own worst enemy. He hates out of prejudice. He hates out of narrow-mindedness. He hates out of stupidity.

She hates out of fear. She hates out of ignorance. Cocked the trigger, the terror of fear, muzzle and barrel, based on what you think you know, takes over. Kill the enemy that causes you pain. Take him or her out—your neighbor, the kid down the street, fellow students on campus—an invasive procedure, but it cuts it out of you.

A shaved pussy, takes centerfold.

Dicks are splashed, across the front of the Exposure, a tabloid newspaper.

Humanures have devolved into sub-humans inhuman. What was life is devalued, marked down. Nothing is sacred anymore.

Killing with lethal accuracy, bloodletting, splashed across trashy junk,

defined as high-powered weapons, which is currency in exchange for a senseless, meaningless, heartless, soulless, end game.

It's the redundant fucking match: who can out-fuck who? Fucking and fucking, numbing and deadening, the drugged fucking contest, perverse twisted fuckers, fucking each other to death, until there is no love,

there is no peace, there is no dignity. The misogynistic whore-mongers,

warring and killing, voyeuristic fucking. It kills innocence, kills children,

kills humanity, and kills the earth.

Kihl is pedaled and sold to the highest bidder. Coming out of the jungles of Spamerica or from the labs of a high-powered drug company, there is one ulterior motive, President Oblaba's hidden agenda. He's on the hellthcare bandwagon, slugging it out with his fellow goons, looney tunes in drag.

John, is banging, the number one prostitute.

That old whore, Dow Jones,

the cash cow, moneymaker, gets gang raped.

Fully loaded, pill poppers are tabulated.

Riveted to the bottom line,

the payoffs and cover-ups accrue.

Trillions in revenue comes at a price.

Blood baths are instigated, promoted and executed. Legislators, mob bosses, kingpins, prime ministers and presidents, are cozy with one another.

Salacious hunger drives them. Greed consumes them.

Power slaughters.

Bystanders witness.

Propaganda intrudes.

A seamless uniformity of distrust and dishonesty is all pervasive as hypocrites defile and defame, so a weakened constitution, makes Spamerica and the whole world, frail and fragile, backward-thinking, on the slippery slope of extinction, sliding into the great, shoreless reservoir called futility.

Meanwhile, Mexiraq's El Don Hubbub is talking to his board about Kihl. "We have to step up production. You know, the old G.O.P. (Gobblers Oldsters Pricks), democratic way of doing things: supply and demand and the U.$.A. demands more. They buy our drugs and supply us with guns.

It's a kill/kill, win/win situation, which we are going to capitalize on."

Shoppers and coppers,

plotters and planners wage a war of consumption. Bland and benign,

your A-game (Apathy,) has you falling asleep, at the wheel as you crash and burn.

They found you with your calendar

between your butt cheeks as you died trying to memorize your laundry list for the day.

And even though your days were numbered, you had your balls, to the grindstone, manning up to the fact, that your tiger had nothing in the tank, (and we're not talking about sperm count).

Kihl on your breakfast cereal had you acting like a dwarf hamster on steroids, racing around in the image of El Don Hubbub. Your drudge count was through the roof, causing you to have strangulated gonads and weakened heart.

Drop it. Tune in. Turn on.

"Ungohdt and your Dr. Summon's alias, whoever you are," Dohg interjects. "Where are you going with your eclectic, aesthetic repertoire?

"You want to show people, how to, "Convert Stress to Power" You're always coming at me from left field. I never know what you're going to spring on me next. I have to say, it's a wild ride, and I guess I'm on board, whether I like it or not. Myotopians? Where the hell did you come up with that? That's really!"

Myopic and squashed up against mountains of junk—as opposed to a cop esthetics—getting loaded up on gargantuan proportions of overload, starving, morbidly, grotesquely;

the emaciated rail, in the middle of an adipose swamp; can't find your wee wee, but you can effortlessly suck your nipples, in a man boob display of the skinniest, two-legged whale, living on box cars of "think thin" wafers

in the latest weight loss craze, for the fattest skinners, hiding under the hide of a gigantic Pillsbury dough boy marshmallow—or something like that.

"I'm starting to get your drift," Dohg says. "But you have to simplify it, so we mere mortals, can understand, what you're saying."

"You're right," Ungohdt says. "I have to try and simplify the language. This has got to be a playbook. In the theater of the damned, sandwiched in between a rock and a hard place, between the devil and trivial details, self-indulged, self-serving, ego junkies shack up with the tone deaf, fat lady who can't sing a note, let alone on key.

Scarf and barf
in a physical finite world
of prodigious overload.
Dead and buried
under the weight of original junk,
shooting your wad in your self-interred,
slaughterhouse junkyard,
where heaven looks like
a giant banana split,
a caloric bloodbath as you die
unhappily and unloved.

I'm inventing, a whole other language. Ah, sweet play! A passageway to uncensored freedom, encoded and at the same time, deciphering wisdom based purely on 'not knowing.'

Inhalers of junk 'got junked.'

Ingested, digested, the junkyard humanures pile it on. The myopic disposition is a constipated society.

Lots of gas and impacted matter, crap backed up to their eyeballs; it can turn the world into a shitty place.

All that gas and matter presses against, the average humanure's low back and now they have sharp, stabbing back pain.

Eighty million people live in denial. They don't want to give up their shit. They are carrying around, a mother load and they either don't want to or don't know how to let go. And the pain is an outcry from the heart of the humanures, telling them to (this is my latest, don't get mad Dohg, but this is it, this is their way out), 'Drop it. Tune in. Turn On.'

"Drop it", which is, the garbage.

Stop being hoarders and whores, get out from under the junk.

"Tune in", to the supreme player who runs the show.

And "Turn On", to the spirit guider, uplifting you into the everlasting play of non.

seaturtlenation@gmail.com

Myotopian Society

High glossies with howitzer brain stems splash across the cover.

Magazines are emptied as killer spreadsheets, do the math.

Twats on ice spread.

The peep show rag makes a killing.

Dick's and pussy's junk out.

It's all there.

Newsstand fucking in racks

hits the killing floor.

Tits and asses get thrown into the mix. "Trysting for a fix," a one night lay,

and then play the field of strays,

rolling in the hay,

waking up to a stranger the next day. Boozing and binging,

lowers the bar on stupidity.

Sex gets devalued, marked down,

"War zoned, fogged in, rape artist

on a thrill-ride power trip,

pop culture kills her, it, them,

misogynist rappers,

heads in the crapper,

flappers, kidnappers,
trophies on a mantle,
hooky monster's abuse,
soulless violators invade.
Fuck, grind out
the fucking disconnect,
degenerate, silver screen idol,
Hellywood's blockbuster
        pillages and mangles,
tangled celluloid strangles
the newfangled starlet,
entangled in glitz and glamor,
her heart crushed
by the jingle jangled hammer.
Love is a whore.
The fucking pyre
burns hotter than hell.

The battleground for market share violently and aggressively attacks.

Mannequin killers, catwalk,
beefed up stick figure junkies
lick the brown sugar spoon,
driving the needle into their tongue.
Moneymakers prostitute.

Fuck heads whore.
Soulless, perverted neon, flash
The sticker price fashioned
into an arsenal of killer designs,
junk in the trunk and hung packages,
plastered on billboards,
flossed and glossed over.

The xenophobia of a Myotopian society is contagious.

Spamerica has jumped ahead of the pack.
The inbreeding of hate is genetic.
Cookie-cutter genomes get cultured.
Purpose is hobbled.
It's a one-dimensional, tunneled shit hole.

Life begins in a Petri dish. Its sugar coated outer shell, with goodie-two-shoes and Motherfucker, compromises hell.

Like laboratory rats in a race against time, spinning their wheels on a virtual reality treadmill.

Mammalian, feathery, upstanding citizens
Plow into the sand, head first.
The escape mechanism
is neither Pavlovian nor Freudian.
Certainly a Jungian animus

cannot explain its straight and narrow,
rigid intolerance to change.
The ostrich-like behavior is done with the eyes open.
Sand scratches the cornea.
Bloodshot and blinded,
the 'vice age' is born,
critters litter and flitter and flaunt
and then vamp and vaunt into inevitable dissolution.
A redeemer collects.
The tab, on borrowed time, has to be paid back,
in full, to the lender.

Ungohdt plays his reed instrument, closes his eyes, just enjoying the moment, lost in reverie.

Ungohdt's House of Disbelief

Dohg cups his hands, over his ears, like in the shape of a conch shell and listens to the mellifluous wave sounds, vibrating in his ear, in his head, feeling his heart chakra open like a lotus blossom.

"You sound like a mad scientist. Which side of the bed did you get out of today? I get the thing with play. Dohgs probably invented it. I hate to burst your bubble, but I have no idea who's going to buy your crap, but you don't care. And this "Drop it. Tune in. Turn on." When did this all come about? The concept is solid, but is it believable?"

Ungohdt stops playing his instrument, walks into his dwelling and places the reed on a cedar table in the middle of the room. He then walks outside and looks toward Dohg.

"It's unbelievable!" Ungohdt says. "And that's what I want to present: the unbelievable. And play, is the glue holding it all together. In Ungohdt's House of Disbelief, no one's 'got god.' Disbelievers are few and far between.

It's a rare breed. They don't squander their time, believing in idolatrous nonsense. Organized religion today is a farce. 'To believe is to deceive.'

To be walled in by belief is so narrow and self-limiting.

"You're nuts!" Dohg exclaims. "Ungohdt's House of Disbelief? You've really lost it this time. Who in their right mind is going to understand that, especially 'QQ (Queer Quacked)', rooting for blabbering Blabber T-Rump, Swamp King, King Con FYI "Crooked Don" shoving his junk down the gullets of his birdbrain constituents—that's what I call humanures. Living inside a belief-hardened outer shell, they have 'the empties' written all over them. In other words, thinking outside the box is something they do not comprehend. Being "off-grid" is so foreign to them it's like an alien from another planet. They just don't get it.

Banging around inside that desolate, empty rat trap, on their virtual reality treadmill, is all they know. Take them outside their comfort zone and they wouldn't survive." He uses a stick to draw his design on the earth.

"Please Dohg," Ungohdt pleads, "leave my bipedal,

anal retentive xenophobes alone.

Round bellied gods, bearded gods, black gods, white gods, yellow gods, brown gods, coming across the border, where gods are defined by the good book they read, prophets, sons of gods, martyrs, collectively looking for a better life,

with believers believing in them, scripture in different tongues, gospel, the truth as defined by a god,

going by the book of belief—it eventually wears thin. The ice breaks and all those skaters fall into the proverbial freeze frame, blood bath."

He looks pensively at the palms of his hands as though seeing something in a mirror, suddenly oblivious to anything going on around him. Dohg tries to talk to him, but Ungohdt doesn't hear anything he is saying. It's as though only Dohg's lips are moving.

Ungohdt rolls down WHAD ST. in his double decker red bus. He reads excerpts from his writings through his blaring bull horn while Dohg drives. Crowds line the street, cheering and wildly applauding.

"'Thou shalt love thy neighbor as thyself;' NOT!" Ungohdt bellows through his bull horn. "That's an altruistic idea, and it has fallen flat on its face. We're at each other's throats, 'Brother against brother, kill or be killed.' This is the tug-of-war that has devolved out of belief. I like that word, devolves, because that's where humanures have headed.

"They are breeding hatred.

It blows out the immune system. It literally crashes.

Brains have become static, hardened from overuse, not plastic, pliable and resilient.

Hearts, having sixty times the amplitude of the brain,

disconnect stall and stop beating

“This is your typical static drudgery.

A system gone haywire

self-implodes and ultimately self-destructs.

Conviction convicts the convicted.

Believers turn victim. Medikill steps in to seal the deal.

Rabid crusaders, marching to the beat of the same ol’ exhaust, burn out from overuse and abuse,

a redundant, repetitive, disorder,

out of balance and out of whack with the environment, with god and the universe. They are trying to validate the killing,

they are trying to score on the big board as an internal die-off, ten trillion friendly bacteria

perish at the hands of a toxic, massive, prescribed, nuclear overdose, the digestive track

turning it into a sterile graveyard.

“Now an army of virulent kill cells invade.

They shut down the immune system. The DNA of a cell feeding on drudge, out of synch with normal cells,

writes a program of invasiveness. Adaptability is shot.

Exhausted and worn out, the believer is brittle and frail there is a loss of elasticity and flexibility.

Stress is dammed up, blocked,

the natural flow of things breaks down.

Stress, like a river of energy, teeming with life, is diverted, shut down, overused and overworked.

The waters become muddy, the flow is interrupted, and balance is compromised.

It degrades and degenerates.

Fallow fields, once rich in nutriments,

become susceptible to degradation. Mutated cells turn cancerous.

They receive a distorted signal from rogue cells, anti-matter positrons, armed with nuclear transmitters,

which codify annihilation.

“Humanures are now wired for self-termination.

The overriding unrest, distress, sleeplessness,

exhaustion and uneasiness (dis-ease) permeates. It’s a believer’s own worst nightmare as the busy signal inside and out (cell phones, electronics, microwaves) reinforces and affirms a tireless battery of invasive forces, wearing them down and wearing them out.

Prostrating on a rug, kneeling on a pew,

or rocking at the Wailing Wall doesn't change anything.

'"I'm not there!' Ungohdt is nowhere to be found in that divisive, overcrowded space, where you're trying to catch your breath, catching up with a god that just isn't there. The space is vacant.

"Here comes a believer with a 'good book' in hand, quoting scripture, the ephemeral, versus the timelessness of infinite wisdom, failing to see their own failings."

Dohg, coyly regains his composure and facetiously replies, having parked their red double decker bus, on the top open floor of a parking garage, next door to the theater Ungohdt is going to rent. As they make their way down, an unlit staircase Dohg continues in his inimitable way.

"You sound like such a genius. I mean all that knowledge. Where did you go to school, Harvard Medical School, Mayo Clinic or Stanford?"

"Dohg, I hate when you get sarcastic," Ungohdt says. "It doesn't suit you. There are more constructive ways to find fault with what I'm saying. Anyway, none of those higher institutions of learning have any idea of what I'm talking about. In all their libraries they haven't the foggiest. They don't have a clue. "

"A super inflated ego, is like a run-away train!" Dohg replies. "Ungohdt, get off it. You don't have all the answers. Look what a mess your humanures have made of their world. What do you have to say for yourself?"

"There you go again gnawing on me like I was an old bone you buried in the yard and just dug up again.

These are my observations.

Dead ends start to pile up. The domino effect propels. Society's downward trend has turned once again

into a slippery slope.

Death begins to phase in as life slips away.

On the brink of a disaster, painfully, it seems incomprehensible that you could expire as the time draws nearer.

Was mediocrity a possible cause? And what is mediocrity?

A risk proof, normal, safe, unchanging, predictable humanure, hollow and empty on the inside, too busy to see or think outside the box, controlled and managed and purposeful, devoid of play."

"That's scary," Dohg says. "You mean to say that's what mediocrity is? That's a death sentence. And there is absolutely no play? How dark and dreary.

"You know something? Here's some insight into that. A cloud hanging over D. C. (Dullards of Collusion), is actually an upside down swampy climate hanging over whitey's house of ill-repute like a crackerjack box moneymaker. The sellout is obvious. Saccharine ass-kissing, bowing and scraping, knee jerk unquestioning obsequiousness to Cirque de Folly, the gelded dyed hair stallion, an apprentice of Vlad the Impaler, hell's stinky little varmint, becomes a sudsy overplayed soap opera. Closed circuit fellatio is carried out by chump mooches. West wing phobia's, eat His junk 24/7.

The diabolically scheming, unchecked violence, behind the scenes, always presenting to the world a normal, safe face, is the workings of redundant mediocrity.

"Then the underbelly is exposed, like raising the debt ceiling. It's a rape artist parlaying their odds to skim and scam.

Of course for profit, what else?
There is hate and a murderous campaign
to kill and destroy anything that gets in your way.
That vile ambition knows no bounds, has no limits

in its power grab, invading, occupying and subjugating.

Is that where Spamerica is heading? The U.$.A. propaganda machine, spewing out that same kind of hate,

but disguised as a demagogue's franchise, the branding of the U.$.A.,

a T-Rump junk, super store, getting the rest of the world to buy into junk imperialism and colonialism, but packaged and labeled as freedom, heartburn, hyperbolic patriotism and tribalism democracy, a trans-fat, overcooked, too much salt, sugar, insatiable empty calories and there we have it: the most exportable commodity, Canadastan's pork belly burgers with lots of kihl for seasoning.

"The tweaking of Spamerica is the main headliner.

And now for the perfect mouthpiece, that is President Oblaba. A rhetorical wordsmith, sharpening the tools of his trade, his machination, poll-driven politicking has the humanure population

marching off a cliff as he bails out, the criminals running his administration.

Pedagogues bogged down

by duplicity and double dealing, terror junkies

shooting up the president, with dry gun powder.

White powder terror, cut with pure, high quality,

weapons grade kihl."

Ungohdt shakes his head in disbelief.

"Dohg, you are getting too cynical. You better have some evidence to back up what you're saying. Or you'll end up in a Gulag, otherwise known as Guantánamo, without any rights, with no habeas corpus your personal freedom just got flushed down the toilet. They're going to label you an enemy combatant and will get your ass locked up. They throw away the key. And your razor wire civil rights get shredded.

"Oblaba plays sissy politics," Dohg insists. "A girly, let-me-hold-your-hand politics, but like any power-grabbing junkie, he has got to get his fix too."

"That's not going to sit well with the CIA (Cocky Idiots Ax (to grind)). Boy are they going to go after you! I got a hold of the declassified, official report on

ground zero. They dropped the ball in a major way. They took an oath to protect and defend and they failed to do that. They all should step down. That would be the honorable thing. Or else they should all be pink slipped, I mean, 'Clean out your desk, you're fired!' Well, they formed a yellow line; cowards protecting their own investments, serving their greedy avaricious needs."

"We better get the show on the road," Dohg says. "I do not want to get caught in that gridlocked traffic-jam. I know you're above it all—always doing your restobics, exercising your inner sanctum 'in the most pristine form of repose,' in your sanctuary, where it's all play. I hate to burst your bubble, but to tell you the truth I think my people invented restobics.

"Humanures, on the other hand, get the 'no pain no gain' washboard brain results as their hearts explode on the last lap in their race against time. What a losing proposition. They think it's good. They are too busy, and too bloated, puffed up and inflated, by their own self-importance. If there was such a thing as a 'stupid pill' they would be the first to corner the market.

"They live in a world of seamless, proprietary, patented vice. It's similar to Chinese torture, but instead of one drop at a time, they ratchet up rigidity and inflexibility in tiny increments, one baby step at a time. It's gridlock with screws. A virtual vice, tightening the screws, heads packed with dates and times, inextricably tied to their own agenda. The language of exclusion overrides everything: a calendared matrix tics; triple espressos, Fanny Buttheads

starring Buck's Forstarters in a café schlock, meteoric, corporate marketing terrorist's hostile takeover.

The squeeze is on. Juicing on caffeine, causing steroidal, hardened brains, morphing biceps into devolved ruptured pythons,

muscling into the pumped-up ego blasts of generic injury prone mediocrity.

"Russian roulette with a vice and a warrantless, wiretapping program tracks the victim.

A de facto gun to the head, vice grips, the trigger is squeezed, bullets whiz by the junkyard wreckage.

They're on a roller coaster ride, a shock wave of highs and lows, peaks and valleys, buzzing with a busy signal.

"And food additives fuel the self-absorbed, an all-consuming firestorm, a chemical blitz of over-dosing and binging.

"The level of unrest escalates.

Armed with a safe, locked, overloaded, normal brain is like a mental piggy bank, filled with plug nickels that can't buy their way out of lockbox lock up. Doing time is the punishment, while not living life is the crime. How do you find yourself? An oxygen debt kills.

"Installments on the payoff are in arrears.

A circumstantial deadline terminates. Playing virtual handball, the heart hits a wall, shorts out and dies. They are Medikill Science's favorite prey;

Overload Quasi has just rented space in the OR (Operating Room). His lease is about to run out.

Dr. Mo Ozzie, sawbones aficionado, is in The House. He saw's his patients' breast bones in half. Carnage and butchery gets billed. Insurance companies hedge their bets. Payola is rampant. The elective BRCA gene gives sawbones the right to exculpatory rape! Radical hysterectomies, mastectomies are done routinely. Medikills predation is unconscionable!

It's a drug corps, crack whore industry. Jacked up prices are shot into veins.

Big biz, is the brains of the operation.

Valve jobs, are a dime a dozen.

Porker valves get a heart that oinks, with each beat. Shove ye old ticker back into the chest cavity. They sew, you back up like a thanksgiving turkey and you're good as new. Actually, it's been slated by the bookies as a Las Vegas long shot. Your chances of survival are 51/50, which is actually a code red, as you are read your last rights. An institutionalized whack-o with industrialized valves, malfunctions, like an over-wound clock, adding up to 101% of gross victimization.

Humanures' heart chakras are like vestigial organs that have no function. They short out. The energy center turns into a drudge pit; not firing on all cylinders, the jalopy, which once hummed in unison, sputters and dies.

"Cocked, locked and loaded, head shot junkies junk out, truncated and slated for guinea pig suicide. "They didn't even bother reading the label as they self-induce the expiration date.

"Caught between a rock and a hard place, the panicky, anxiety-ridden, Viagra-driven, hard on, hemorrhages; going blind and impotent is the medikill textbook definition of 'side effects'.

"Attachment has them flat-lining as they live in ruse control, in a defensive posture of biased rigidity. With crash and burn on the horizon, they up the dosage. Overdosing is habitual. So Joe the bartender and Madge the meter maid, wash up on the shore of Medikill Science's hospital beaches; they are checked in, comatose signing away on the dotted line all their rights, so they can be scheduled for corporeal reconfiguration and reassignment. Roomed and boarded, probed and pried, they flounder like fish out of water. Hook line and sinker, they swallow the bait.

White coats throw the switch and hitch them up to the nuking fryer. Shriveled gonads, a heart looking like overcooked spam, and a brain like a deep fried Twinkie—

the invasion was a success,

but the patient's died.

"Selfotomies are performed routinely, either by submissive injection or by removal of the pineal gland, 'the seat of the soul' (according to Descartes). The third eye is blinded, so the blind, blind the blind and lead them to imperceptible blindness. The scarred, cauterized un-self has no self-left.

"Less-self, more drugs and invasive procedures: the hair trigger response that Medikill Science is looking for. Dr. Killjoy and his hordes of Faustian choppers and cutters, shooters and painkillers, line up for a crime that fits the punishment, prognosticating diagnoses.

"Cutters and shockers, in an ex-rated, invasive procedure, leave only hair follicles and scrotum, to show that they are in full control of their faculties."

With the landlord's permission, Ungohdt has gained entry to the theater he's going to rent, through the back stage door, in an alley right next door to the parking garage. He's standing on stage, while Dohg sits up front. He puts the bull horn he is carrying down in a corner of the stage.

"You have really out done yourself," Dogh says. "I mean, did you swallow a funny bone and now I have to hear your Laugh Factory stand-up routine? *This* is torture!"

Suddenly a loud noise comes from the front of the theater. Whoever it is, they are making a racket.

It turns out to be the Siamese twins, police chiefs, Mickey "Cone-head" Schlemiel and Manfred "Gallstone" Carny, goons of the Spamerica cabal. They are joined at the lips and also at the genitals—in other words they share one penis between the two of them.

They happen to also have the same set of vocal chords, so they speak in one voice, a voice scratchy and barely understandable, raspy and dissonant, they bark out their demands like barkers at a circus. They are a walking, talking, sidestepping freak show. They hold a piece of paper and in a screechy tone say, "Dr. Summon, you are under arrest for violating our ordinances and you have not obtained a business license to operate this theater. There is a bench warrant issued for your

arrest. You are in violation of the laws of eminent domain." Ungohdt seems unperturbed by their demands.

"You haven't a leg to stand on," he tells them. "I have every right to be on that land and as far as a business license we have already applied for one. I will help the Manhattoes to reclaim what is rightfully theirs."

The Carnies hold onto a leash. At the end of it is a hogena, wearing a barbed wire choker, pulling violently on it and lunging forward viciously. It looks ready to tear Ungohdt limb from limb.

Meanwhile the pukka Dohg (that no one can see, including the police chiefs) prepares to do battle with what he sees as the enemy.

The hogena is color blind, but it can see the shadowy figure of the pukka as he stands up and makes himself visible to the hogena. He changes into a saber tooth tiger and roars so loud it's deafening. The hogena's fierce yapping turns into a whimper as it hides behind the police chiefs.

Realizing something has gone terribly wrong they look out over the theater seats, but can't see anything.

They seem to change their tune. "Okay, where is that pukka you claim to have? We don't think it even exists. No one has seen it. You're playing a trick on us. We'll get even. We have the law on our side. You and the Manhattoes are history. It's curtains for all of you!"

They back off and retreat through the theater doors.

Ungohdt looks at Dohg. "Good job. You scared them off. You pulled the rabbit from the hat and turned that hogena into a pussycat. Come on, let's get out of

here, before they come back. Let's leave through the back stage door." Ungohdt and Dohg quickly exit from the theater and make their way back home.

Ungohdt and Dohg have narrowly escaped from the clutches of the dastardly police chiefs. They sit quietly inside their dwelling. For the time being, they are safe and sound.

By candlelight, Ungohdt prepares another edition of his newsletter, *Time to UNWIND*. In it he exposes the most diabolical corporate terrorist, *Basturds Petroleum*. They had drilled for oil off the southern coast of Spamerica, in the Sea of Mexiraq. Con-Us with Oblaba's blessing, had issued them unrestricted licenses to drill in those waters. They had drilled thousands of feet into the sea floor when something went terribly wrong. The 'preventer valve', failed, causing sparks to fly from the force of metal on metal. As the oil and gas gushed out with incredible force, like a huge geyser, a flame as though from the bowels of hell, shot hundreds of feet into the air. The fire destroyed, the oil rig and everyone on board died.

The catastrophic impact, to the environment, was immeasurable. It seemed, that the two, major advocates, for the environment, and especially for the wild life, were Ungohdt and the Manhattoes. There were, relatively small groups of humanures, protesting the oil spill and the environmental devastation. That was

quickly quelled and repressed by the administration, who had just upped, their kihl intake and gave away, truckloads of I-Bone, self-absorbent maxi-pods, the electronic techniques, used for crowd control and appeasement, to smooth things over, so to speak. Bribing the public to dummy up, drugging them, with the opiates for submission as the stock market soared, into the stratosphere of greed and power, overcooking the books. It was like a runaway train; there were no brakes to stop it, no oversight, no checks and balances, just voracious greed, hoarding and accumulating wealth, so it became transparently, gluttonously clear; the rich got much richer and the poor most definitely, got poorer, while the middle class became a classless caste of untouchables, having lost their identity and their significance as major contributors to the wholeness and wellness of society. They had been marginalized and beaten down, losing their faith, hope and dignity.

Ungohdt had demanded that president Oblaba, put a surcharge on every transaction, taking place, in the stock exchange, whether buying or selling. The rank, bald-faced profiteering, had to stop. Someone had to put an end, to the crap- shoot, that was destroying free markets and the global economy. Everyone had to be accountable. Eventually, his proposed program would create prosperity and not austerity, if those in power would just listen and reign in and oversee the program Ungohdt, had written about. Of course it seemed futile and it was probably, falling on deaf ears, but someone, had to step up to the plate and put their life, on the line and take a stand.

'The Vice Age', teeters on extinction as it lists to one side, the ship was sinking. The Plan-it Kill bender; headed up by El Presidente "Crooked Don" T-Rump. Emolument violator, the ships' floating crap game, had T-Rumps trademark boorish brand, artless fleecing. Stacks belched out, 'huge' amounts of soot and hydrocarbons, into the atmosphere.

"Oops—the boat sprung a leak! Gunk, rupture through a crack in the fail safe epitaph.

Black gold is frothing

in a sea of death.

Feathery creatures and those wondrous beauty's, breathing through gills,

dying by the millions;

populations are wiped out.
Genocide goes global.
Turncoat caretakers
pollute their own toxic vessel

with gallons of nonfat milk (one and two percent nonfat): white swill, leaching out minerals, with zero percent nutritional value, poisoning the ecosystem they live in.

The body becomes, a dumping ground
for what becomes, a chemical wasteland.
Toxicity is off the charts.
The rigid, stiff, humanure
makes garbage the staple
of a festering wound
as a stick figure, a child
with a swollen belly,
sifts through, the reeking stench.

The byproduct of greed and unchecked power is, toxic garbage.

The poison seeps into the ground water,
into wells and aquifers,
into every cell and every molecule,
rewriting the DNA,
and from that devolution,
comes the humanure:

not exactly a race,
but more a one-dimensional,
linear, bio-sewer;
a chromosomal consumer,
an over-doer, self-absorbed junky,
in all its permutations.
The humanure, short circuits its mainframe
and overloads the circuitry,
causing stress to distress and then degrade,
so that stress becomes adulterated and tainted.
It no longer is stress, but rather
caked up plaque, insidiously destructive,
the inorganic grime, called 'drudge.'

"That is the precursor to cancer and to any degenerative disease.

The blockhead, unable to adapt,
crushed in mountains of stuff, succumbs.
Calling up the same overused,
tired, worn out, habitually prompted, 'needs to do.'
Overdone the abuser pushes empty calories
and lethal, gargantuan amounts
of toxic self-inflicted;
the appetite craves
killing: killing feeling, killing pain,

killing anger, killing fear;
shutting down the monster,
fomenting and morphing, into a killer.
Morbidly obese,
the chow hound digs his or her, own grave.
Inside the all-you-can-eat walk in,
his habit takes over—
not out of hunger, but out of want and need,
consuming until he goes with
the lap band procedure;
he doesn't have the stomach for
real change as he trades one addiction,
for another, fucking himself to death
in cheap motels and shooting up in back alleys."

Ungohdt pretends, that he has taken, center stage as he stands on his head and recites, out loud, his monologue. When he pauses, Dohg takes the opportunity, to interrupt and put in his two cents, while he is morphing into giant koala.

"Standing on your head, is certainly a novel way of turning the gravity of the situation, upside down," Dohg observes. "Ungohdt, careful with all that blood, rushing to your head—you might have an apoplectic moment as you slur and slurp your soup-to-nuts rendition of salvation.

"You're a real power broker. You use leverage, like someone opening a can of beans with a crow bar." Ungohdt seems unfazed, by Dohg's sarcasm as he continues to rib Ungohdt, who just laughs it off. "Hey, I am not being disrespectful. I have the highest admiration for you. But your way of proving a point, can be laborious and somewhat tedious. Let's put a good dose of virtual reality, back into our saving-the-world-scenario."

Ungohdt, still standing on his head, closes his eyes and takes a deep breath, seemingly in a state of meditation. Nothing seems to phase him, especially Dohg.

"The steering wheel, in your ear

is a committee of one, listening to your own chicken shit crew, going up the river to serve out their life sentences behind the bars of the limited edition U.$. A. cellblock. (Unholy $tate of Apathy)

It's a paperless, electronic shooting match, shot up with the junk of the day. The bidding war has begun. The killing is fully operative.

A well-oiled killing machine
rolls onto the battlefield,
numbers flash, prices slash,

automatically, a huge arsenal of cash,
moves across the grid,
severed limbs, are unidentified,
bowels, laid out, on the floor.
Spilling your guts out,
the fight goes on until the closing bell,
when profits and losses are tallied.
It's a war, so who really wins?
Loses go unnoticed.
The stats pile up.
The body count climbs and headless torsos,
are thrown into a dumpster.
They didn't have a chance to satisfy their indebtedness.

A sea of red tape is like, a red tide of
the unwashed dried blood,
absorbed by the 'stop the presses',
tabloid spread of inconsolable death and dying.
To print wars, freezes time in a recyclable tragic history."

"For some reason," Ungohdt replies, "I think you like to kick me when I'm down. I might be wrong. If so I will apologize.

BPST *(Basturds Petroleum Scoundrel Trial*)

Judge Angelips Jowly Judge Angelips Jowly slams the gavel numerous times, trying in vain, to quiet down her courtroom. It is so loud she can't hear herself think. She usually runs a tight ship. She doesn't tolerate any nonsense. If she thinks you're out of order, she'll slam her gavel like a sledge hammer and throw the book at you. "You're in contempt of court and so I am fining you, five thousand dollars and you'll also do forty five days, in county jail!" "But your honor…" the defendant replies. She cuts her off…"I don't want to hear it!" and has the bailiff take her away.

Today is a rather unusual day. She has in her court Dr. Summon—AKA Ungohdt—and the chief of Manhattoes, Rodney Eaglewing, who has filed a class action suit, in superior court, at city hall, on Wall St., against BP (Basturds Petroleum). They are the plaintiffs, charging the corporate terrorist giant, with destroying Long Island Sound wetlands and wanton slaughtering wildlife, in particular Ellen the Pelican and her offspring, eggs that were in her nest, destroyed by the toxic oil spill. It has also impacted the fisheries. As a result of the toxic spill, small businesses lining the coast, whether fishermen or restaurants or bait shops, have been closed down. Thousands have lost their jobs.

Contamination of the waters and fishes' food source, by BP has recklessly and deliberately destroyed the natural habitat, killing off possibly millions of those who were part of Sea Turtle Nation. Their voices, their lives and those of their offspring, have been needlessly sacrificed and silenced, for one thing and one thing only; the bottom line, money, "record profits" driven by rampant, unchecked greed.

Ungohdt (AKA Dr. Summon) has gotten airplay, on pirate radio, with his song, "Ellen's Song", a tribute to Ellen and her plight, trying to save her nest and her eggs, her children to be and all wildlife destroyed by the toxic oil spill. Also playing is "Peace IS Alive" and "Whad St.", considered the greatest, contemporary political satirical song of our times. He is gaining traction. People are listening and surprisingly buying his CD. His audience keeps growing.

Hubbub and his henchman and cronies hate the fact that Ungohdt and the Manhattoes are actually getting some traction.

Judge Angelips Jowly screams at the top of her lungs, "Quiet In the courtroom! Quiet in the courtroom!! I will not tolerate such insolent behavior. Dr. Summon, Ungohdt, whoever you are, you are the cause of turning my courtroom in a free-for-all. I have read your complaint. Who or what is *Sea Turtle Nation?* I have never read anything so preposterous." Between her six-inch-long false eyelashes and

botox, steroidal enhanced lips and bulging, bloodshot dark brown eyes, she spits out her contempt for Ungohdt and his fellow supporters, seated behind her bench. In her black robes, like the wicked witch of the east, she lets you know, that she rules. "And this pukka of yours, one that only you can see and hear—is he or she or it in the courtroom? Or is this just a figment of your twisted imagination?" Of course

her scurrilous hatred, for the plaintiff is obvious.

Ungohdt responds, "Yes, my pukka is with me. He is a

soul mate, a truly glorious creature. I don't appreciate your rancor and acrimonious attack, against him and I might add, against me. It is unjustifiable. Anyway, you should have recused yourself, due to the fact that there is a conflict of interest here. You were sitting on the bench for the city suing us for the eminent domain issue. In that case we were the defendants."

The judge seems very agitated. She stands up, glares at Ungohdt directly in the eyes. Her heated response is telling. "How dare you question my authority?!, I was appointed by the city and have the absolute AUTHORITY, to judge the eminent domain case or this one as well. I am about to find you in contempt of court Dr. Summon!!!"

It's the middle of the day and Ungohdt is on the corner of Whad St. and Broadway, holding a stack of his newsletter, shouting, "EXTRA, EXTRA, read all about it!" He then extemporaneously recites his prose.

"Slaughtering, one another, is stylized, gentrified and justified.

The unyielding fog stiffens.
War totters of guns, fogged in.
Kill. Just following orders
Decorated heroism, is shot full of holes.
The tattooed, 'stupid' sign
on your forehead, says everything.
The headlining of the maimed and dying
is obscured.
Heroes goose step to Mein Trumph.
Battle fatigued flash backs reveal
the massacre.
Hung out to dry, mass graves bury feelings.
The beginning of the end, draws from futility.
Desperation, has nowhere to go.

A chamber of horrors, like a room full of carnival mirrors,

stares death in the face.

It distorts and mangles.

Lost inside what you don't know.

Your shelf life is short lived.

You outlived your expiration date.

Living on borrowed time dissipates.

"The newest IPO, Terrorizeme Inc., exploits and demonizes. The privatization of war, has turned into a no-bid bidding war. The tax-free, offshore investment, has El Presidente "Crooked Don" T-Rump, cashing in his stock options. After all, he was once their CEO. He was given stock options as part of his hiring bonus. T-Rump Incorporated, is a privately owned company of the U.$.A., whose pals in high places, namely, Bushwhack and Ambush, have garnered the favor of these two power brokers. With zero degrees of separation from him and his much publicized border wall, he nationalizes cultural racism, runs his campaign on skinhead "Duke" nativism, while jingoism ranting and ravings exacerbates his incurable MLPD (Multiple Liar's Personality Disorder). His bed of liar barbed wire is where he pretends it's actually a bed of roses as he bleeds inwardly hemorrhaging the grotesquely vile lying crap he continuously wallows in.

Inculcating "the terrible two's", the dotard toddler personifies an unprecedented oxymoron.

"The terror is self-inflicted on Plan-it Kill. Stocks soar. Terror is institutional.

Medikill's, backbone servers, prey on gullibility. Preachers and Medikill doctors terrorize.

Chapter and verse, scribbled prescriptions instill fear.

The terror of terror, BS-2, sledge-hammers home, the redundant I.S.I.S. bludgeoning tool, strapped to the T-Rump whipping post. Aggressively marketed, terror is a cocked pistol, in the hands of an eight-year-old, going into his elementary school somewhere in the Midwest, with the intention of killing as many of his classmates and teachers as possible, before he kills himself.

He hit 'the wall.' A dead end tagged.

Shut off and shut down, his violence raged, unnoticed. The pressure cooker boiled over. The death knell tolled.

"And then, there's terror:

an exportable commodity, on every stock exchange, in the world, and if you read in between the lines, it's there in every corporate board room, in every drugstore and gun store, across Spamerica. It's unstoppable.

"Terror masks terror; the brutal unrelenting terror,

fearful of terror, consumed by terror, the social networking finger pointing homogenizes, going public with its blood sport. Farcebook's, Tahrir menu, scrolls down. Kill zone Humanures, jonesing on double clicks, suck on cyberspace, like they're in a Hellywood nitrous oxide bar, anaerobic junkies, shooting up. The results? 'Murder Incorporated.' A cellular raiding party attacks.

"Myotopian blasé—bland, benign, complacent and apathetic—belies the subliminal motive of warfare advertisers.

"An army of Tweeting Tweakers, carping and harping, blindly lash out and kill in the name of the mass's social networker terrors. Cued up, vicarious errorists, clutch their mouse and keyboards, and go viral, in a drooling, wannabe, virtual reality treadmill rattrap.

Terror becomes a global phenomenon.

"Your own worst enemy stares at you, from screaming headlines and hidden crawlspaces. Newsy, pulpy addiction to terror overrides.

seaturtlenation@gmail.com

Your terror Sasquatch, the missing link, bears a surprisingly close

resemblance to you.

"Terror pervades you, invades you.
Media exports terror.
Your mind, imports it.
The hostile takeover images
intrude every waking moment.
Who is the fugitive?
Cut from the same cloth.
Manufactured terror grows exponentially.
Fears multiply. Anger shadows suspiciously.
Suspicions stereotype as subconscious
and conscious mind contort and twist.
Magazines, fully loaded with ammo
for the killing, hit the stock exchange.
The leverage buyout, takes you out!
The slug fest for power and greed
uses terror as leverage.
No bare knuckles. Nobody bleeds.
It's all kept under wraps.
Executed by backroom terrors,
Back pocket executioners
sold out for the right price.

Money whores bill it and you pay for it.
Wake up, Spamerica!!
Evangelistic generals strong-arm the
terrorism mouthpiece, and at the drop of a hat,
he's ready to call in the artillery.
Terrorized by what might be
their Canadastan—preaching war, living war,
consumed by war and from inside
his warhead brain,
like a warhead surgeon, a warhead preacher,
or a warhead teacher, they bomb justifiably.
The terror mechanism,
a knee-jerk reflex.
They kill and cut out and target,
using the playbook on terror,
terrorizing you to death.
The road map to annihilation,
is the 'killer strategy' with no exits.
Once you're in the theater,
there is no escaping.
The attrition of terror and the fodder
    for impending slaughter,
are now asking the age old question,
'Why are we here? What's the point?

Where are we going with this?'
And the deafening silence,
does not answer
because there is no answer
to a rigid, inflexible mindset,
running on, the fossil-fueled fumes,
of a prehistoric deathtrap.
A pernicious decision undermines
and, at the same, time controls.
Proselytizing missionaries of terror invoke fear.
A faceless jihad,
based on a gridlocked road map,
the ravages of terrors and pathology.
Treacherous gods on pedestals,
cut out and exterminate.
Painkillers offer salvation.
Miscreants drugged on religious fervor
are hard wired
to an 'improvised explosive deviant' (I.E.D.),
a self-prescribed war.
If you want to go to heaven,
kill everything that feels and kill every emotion.

"Lucifer's ghouls, are strung out, on the genesis of hate,

a religious doctrine, written with the blood of innocents.

The rape artist's
strip club on capitol hill,
is suited up with poll dancers,
dancing around the issues,
amounting to a hill of beans.
Bean counters, legislating
lock up; dead ends intersect.
Traffic jams the virtual gridlock,
a battlefield with no exit signs.
The stalemate kills.
Polarized,
politico junkies drowning in a well
filled with sand, in a theater of the dammed;
'dammed if you will and damned if you won't,'
a bi-partisan screwing session,
in an orgy of screwballs, insolent and indolent,
shafting anything or anyone that moves.

Taxpayers boozing and binging,
all liquored up on bailout, 180 proof.
'Too Big to Fail.' They get their jugular ripped out
and watch it hemorrhage on the killing floor.

Victims don't even know, they're bleeding to death
as they bleed green, and what once was real estate
is all under water. consumed by an over-indulgent appointment with death, the suicidal ambition of droll mediocrity is her 'noose of no return,' sticking her neck out one last time, with zero risk factor.

"An unlit staircase of confusion leads to nowhere. A poetic conclusion might help, but there is no poetry and no love when locked into a hollow, solitary confinement, unable to think for yourself.

The wonder of play and the dream of play is destroyed as the child dies out of neglect, abuse and or violation."

Know-its of Whomsday

"Dohg," Ungohdt says, "I am not trying to be a shrink. Give me a break. After all, I am Dr. Summon, and I should have some idea of what's going on in Spamerica. Look, killing is pandemic. It's a worldwide, incurable miasma. That's why I brought the non to Manhattan. We have grown a rainforest here—unheard of until now—and we are introducing new ways, to create bio fuels for clean energy. I mean, solar synthesis by itself is a major breakthrough. Imagine how many jobs that will create. We are stoking the fires of change. Like I said, it's an uphill battle, but if we stay with it, we will reap what we sow.

"And do not forget our art deco theater that we are now renovating. Visually and aesthetically, we are creating another industry. The Repose Lounge is at the forefront of what holistic healing is about." Ungohdt pauses for a moment and then extemporaneously recites, his prose and poetry to himself as he so often does.

"Like a street urchin, wandering aimlessly,

abandoned and unloved, orphaned by circumstance. Buried under a storied past, the rosy future seems implausible. The inexhaustible, tireless energy, being in the moment, scares you. Too intense and too impassioned, it can make you pliable and malleable. And so the present becomes life's stage."

Dohg seems distracted. He is not listening too closely to what Ungohdt has to say. Pukka that he is, he stretches his neck like a giraffe so to eat the seeds of the non-trees on higher branches.

"You really have a thing for the now. You and Baba Ram Das got hooked up at the here and now. I have the nose for the here and now. That's even better than you Ungohdt. I mean, I do not think, we'll ever be rivals."

Ungohdt is not paying much attention to Dohg; he continues, seemingly preoccupied.

"It's in the schools," Ungohdt says. "Places of worship, piled up, cellular, steaming masses of protoplasm; thinking and linking, wiping and stripping plastic, laundry lists, ad infinitum, hoarding, abhorring, whoring, but smiling and pretending. Homogenized, the steamy loaves are left by the horseplay. From fodder to digested, factitious warmed-over, hind-sighted alien- entropies, growing out of the seeded clouds of self-doubt and futile posturing, attitudinal hierarchies, preaching and teaching, Myotopian good book, cooking classes; rob, cheat, deceit, lie, hypocrisy, the mainstay of an incurable case of mediocrities. Leveraging against time, but always losing, even though claiming victory, the win, win cliché for selling out has, 'loser' written all over it."

"You just blurted out with that!" Dohg exclaims. "Where do we go from here? You're full of surprises.

You can be so poetic at times and then the prose comes roaring out of you, like verbal diarrhea."

The silence is deafening as Ungohdt prepares to parry and joust with what he playfully refers to as his *alter ego*. "Let's get really crazy, Dohg," Ungohdt excitedly proposes with gusto. "It's the Know-it's of Whomsday!!" Ungohdt says, "We in Hellywood baby! We're on Fairfax near Sunset at the Faux-It-Styx, Rope-A-Dope Theater, and I'm about to get into the ring with the Blacks and Whites of the T. V. show, *I Love It Juicy,* and slug it out, in a unicolor shooting match where everybody looks like homogenized milk. We'll be jawing white bread, soaked in Jim Morrison's "L. A. Woman" memorabilia, collected from his groupies; "Break on Through, to The Other Side". That's just the icing on the cake in what has been affectionately called *Blasé Town*. Get this: they're giving me five minutes to deliver my knock-out shocker. So here we go!!!"

seaturtlenation@gmail.com

Five

Five minutes to catch a plane, to catch a bus,
did my train leave the station?
Who are all these strangers?
Welcome to the dangers of falling flat on your face,
your 300 seconds of fame, just might go up in flames;
or maybe this can be like the movie “300",
where you can stand, on the stage
as King Leonidas, at the Battle of Thermopylae,
surrounded by fellow Spartans, ready to fight to the death.
Canter’s onslaught of deli sandwiches, like Xerxes armies,
precariously piled high,
with mountains of pastrami and corn beef—
would you cut the mustard (poupon, deli mustard or horseradish)?
In your high-flying, high- fiving, attempt at redemption,
failure was not an option, a flotilla of three-mast deserts,
like magnificent ships, listing in the Fairfax sea

of self-gorging and self-indulgence, rocking on the tide of anti-depressants,

antacids and breath mints, outflanked by seeded rye and kosher pickles,

the crash and burn of self-deprecation, took five steps forward

and then five steps back, one canceling out, the other.

The preposterous goose egg, at the end of my aspirations is intolerable,

an elliptical zero maybe just maybe my rolling stone, gathering no moss,

my ticket to freedom as I grab hold of the microphone,

like grabbing hold of the reins

as if I was the fifth horsemen of the apocalypse,

bringing down the house, my poem of revelation, circumventing

all those bad things to bring, to you, to them, to those, Rimbaud vagrants,

my audience applauding wildly

as I ride into the musk-scented path of an enraged bull elephant.

It was like getting run over by a big rig.

Maybe I could start a fifth column, inside the Greenway Court Theater,

rally the troops, to fend off the naysayers, the deaf ears, the blind eyes,

persona non-existent, like home grown terrorists,

they wage their self-war of apathy and complacency,

consuming copious amounts of schlock and shtick,

the habits they can't kick,

mediocrities, at their worst, myopic robotic, cosmetically designed, numb-dumbs,

running on empty, sucking up fumes, the tinsel lifestyle time bombs,

the toxic charms that only cash can buy,

and from that smorgasbord of hoarders and whores,

from the mash pit of da poetry lounge, I will rise like a Phoenix

to plant a kiss, on the lips of the ashen dust particles,

of the politically correct world of excesses and obsesses,

where a mouse and a fact-house, on a virtual reality treadmill,

shoots the double click, cyber-junk making of an inhuman louse.

And so the know-its of Whoms-day herd the gadflies of Fads-way

onto the pinhead buzzer of the five minute replay.

Judge Angel frantically bangs her gavel, like a sledge hammer against concrete, to quiet her courtroom—but to no avail. "Quiet, in the courtroom! Quiet in the courtroom!! I am going to throw you all out of here, including the media, and bar them from coming back into this courtroom. I gave Ungohdt, AKA Dr.

Summon, thirty days for contempt; and rightfully so, I might add." Ungohdt enters

through a side door, accompanied by the bailiff. He takes a seat. He does not have a lawyer. He is representing himself, pro per.

Finally the courtroom quiets down. You could cut the tension with a chainsaw.

Here goes Ungohdt diving into one of his soliloquys. "And of course the Gadflies of Fadsway, a Hellywood universe, with fizzled out start-ups, glamor pus lifestyles, riddled with the not-so-glamorous, humanures drudge, the unvarnished, sewerage,

bonehead celebrity,

honey pots, glam jam, perfumed ham hocks.

Humanures', steaming hot beef cakes, spread all over tabloid headlines, twats and heaved prick hunks,

vomited putrescence, puking fashioned mannequin, spaghetti strapped, flasher posers,

prostituting, whoring, performing, jumping through hoops, trained fleshpots, defile and defame,

for fame and cash, the bling things, flaunt and slink, ostentatious fakers, faking, luster busters, getting uglier and uglier,

who'll be the ugliest, primped, glossed, mag hags, mugging and jawing actors, snorting lines,

a snow white, drugging contest, drinking in the limelight, shot into the eye of the camera flashers,

flashing, dashers dashing, mashing and gnashing, Tom cats spraying, leading men in panties and spiked heels,

and leading ladies wearing the balls of a bull market, slither onto the screen in a novel adaptation of fornication,

a gang banging, vicarious, overlay of box office receipts.

Outside the courtroom the inimitable Dohg interjects. "Let me get my two cents in here," Dohg interjects. "El Don Hubbub and Elvis Judas Krist are the major, super drudge. They go by the PKM (Pathological Killer's Manual): Kill the pain, overkill and overkill in true Kihl fashion, painkillers, on a thrill ride, to good hellth.

Subliminally rigged to blindly kill, invade, violate, rape, pain killed killers, kill over and over again.

“The Jackal, gets locked up, shut away in some dark closet, a cobwebbed attic with no light, closed windows and doors, feeling dismantled, the offspring’s buried alive, populated by Damian's and reruns of *The Omen*; The Exorcist crawls up your ass, looking for the bowels of your soul and ends up eating it, using a cross as a fork, dining on devil do-do. All I can say is that it’s become a shitty affair.

“Morbidly suck eggs, through your nose, so your anorexia, can be supplanted by Medkill’s latest disease, ‘Sucking Eggs Restless Syndrome.’ and somehow, miraculously, Medikill, has come up with, a prescribed cure that kills everything in your body, with one exception: your anus.

“It’s Medikill’s way of prescribing and reinforcing violation.

“Armed with an arsenal of lethal painkillers, they attack and assault, over and over again, affirming the affirmation, symptom kill, the tip of the iceberg, not the cause, a symptom based “kill zone”, until the buy in has no way out, and the believer victimizes the victim, self-killing, self-authorized, signed, sealed and delivered.

“Again and again, eviscerate the pain, cut it out, render it helpless and powerless, detach from it, disengage, disfigure, disassociate, dismember and then, violently kill. At the head of the list of killers are prescribed prescription drugs, designed to repress and suppress, the junky, ‘depression’ masks and buries dead feelings and shuts down until the victim turns into an unrepentant killer, killing for pleasure and deliberately sent into suburban war zones, gentrified ghettos, back alleys stairwells, hiding intruders and invaders, hell bent on killing, lashing out a subconscious, bestial rage; must uncontrollably kill, without feeling, without remorse.

“The uniformed, inmate of the armed forces,
rolls a hand grenade, into a room,
filled with women and children,
‘prepping’ for a sociopath’s,
justifiable, strung-out purpose;
by the book, cold-blooded,
the monster within has every reason to kill
for the sake of killing. It’s a rote, automatic reflex.
An insatiable appetite follows commands.

"The genetic proclivity is there, hidden in the deep recesses of a subconscious mind, consumed by a raw, open wound: unhealed, disquieting, restless anger.

"Authored by white jacketed, stethoscope-hanging, scalpel-wielding, syringe-injecting, Medikill saw bones. Armies of sucker 'diseasoids', binging on the Medikill model, deprogramming and then reprogramming, deviants in a well-oiled sickness machine; the institutional victimization is none other than the Medikill industrial complex.

"Just in case you didn't know what a diseasoid is, let's explain. Your guinea pig, civilian duty to succumb, in total submission, to the shoot-em-up, vaccinated herd of believers, en mass, is a symptom-based slaughterhouse.

Frown's posture, ingesting, on downers and gnarly uppers,

fake an orgasm, and anti-climax parades,
strut their junk,
along death row.
'Strangers in a Strangled Sham',
go into 'grok shock.'
And if you don't get that, that's just too bad.

It's the classic place, between a 'rock and a crack place,'

between the corral and the pen.
Cell block dead end, is an excuse,
for murdering yourself.

Self -immolation is a doctored suicide.
Over-consumption, as in overindulgence,
is the habit of choice.
A plethora of choices, like a spread sheet,
maps out carnal offerings.
An agreement,
N.S.G.C.T.A. (North Spamerican Generic Choices Trade Agreement),
has been signed within the blue zone,
a cyanotic, oxygen-starved environment,
to get the brain, to think in bingo squares,
and the heart to momentarily, stall out,
so that a sudden cardiac death
and an ischemic brain,
can fill up with drudge-squared choice,
simulated microchips
a revolving door,
stacked in favor of static,
unchanged, preprogrammed choices.

The Canadastans and the Mexiraqs, sit at the table of the Unholey $tate of Apathy and sign off on Mousetrap Lane, a North Spamerican, industrial complex, supporting the N.S.G.T.A.

The end results: the poorest get poorer.

The hungry get hungrier.

The rich get greedier.

They corner the market.

They straddle both sides of the equation.

So it's like building, the options market or a hedge fund,

gold brick, by golden parachute.

The Oz of Wall Street

and the escape hatch of Main Street

are called Whad Street.

It's the ultimate in cyber interment.

Lock up never looked so pretty.

Madeoff minds and payoff blinds,

cover up misdeeds.

Babylon in a new millennium,

like the Sodom and Gomorrah of old,

with the resurrection of the Las Vegas strip.

Our beloved, bespectacled Benjamin

reincarnates as king of the slots.

Slotted destinations and a world of choices
What could be better?

Operate at the dizzying heights of bottom feeders.
Feeding on bathtub ring slime,
and the unrecognizable remains of the baby,
that got thrown out, with the bath water,
they cannibalize as the forensic evidence,
points to the mug shot line up,
viewed from, in front of,
the boob tube screen
by the vicarious dunces,
playing stupefied, apathetic victims.
Sitting on the deck
of a makeshift aircraft carrier,
emblazoned on a giant banner,
is the following:
'TOO BIG TO FAIL'; 'MISSION ACCOMPLISHED.'
Gangster bankers go, Bushwhacking
by hijacking the economy and setting in place
a kill zone apparatus
so they can continue making a killing.

The grudge match, is an unsolvable, gang bang, between 'normal and safe', refereed by predictable, the irascible, ugly twins of constipated normalcy, the opiate drudgers, feeding on the glossy drudgery of embalmed lifestyles, (both are the bookends to mediocrity, it's just a question as to which one, is the prettiest oxymoron).

Stereotyping is part and parcel.
A drudger, filled with drudge, is shut down.
It's a safe, normal, overexposed,
kill zone, which best describes it.
Your typical drudger,
eats drudge chips, for breakfast.
Grudgers, range from privates, to generals,
from politicians to doctors and preachers,
from authority figures of the lowest rank
to the highest;
soft pedal, doling out the comfort foods in a
war zone safety net
of self-destruction; a chip off the Bushwhack block.
The tedium of the kill zone is unchanged.
It's the terror of that static world,
that amasses weapons;
weapons in the form of drugs,
weapons in the form of guns;

the final outcome: kill.

"Plan-It Kill is your virtual reality,
a gyroscopic treadmill.
The rat trap and the cyber gridlock
are locked into overload.
The scales are tipped in favor of
overkill, and so death
becomes the arbitrator.
Replacing life was at the heart of degeneration.
Technology is designed, to support redundancy.
Guns and bombs are built to kill.
Drugs are manufactured to kill.
Plan-It kill is, an overbooked kill zone.
Better known as Whomsday,
the general population fragmented into
a pharmaceutical nomenclature,
labeled Know-its,
doubling as the Gadflies of Fadsway,
the monkey-see, monkey-do
of Hellywood's scotch guard, red carpet,
fireproofed beef cakes, their strutting fleshpots,
'floozy's dozy oozy'
of stage, screen and rubberized gonads'

glam pusses, glitzy, mannequin queens.
Like a rhyming Dr. Suess storyboard,
a calendar filled with dates and times,
with atrophied genitals and much smaller minds."

I-Bone

Everyone, and I mean everyone,
is in mass hysteria, clamoring for the I-Bone.
Dial up and just get I-Boned.
Getting screwed in cyberspace is a trip, to say the least.
I mean hanging out,
just you and your I-Bone.
Suppository or sucker,
you insert and it squirts.
an electronic, mechanical self-fucker.
Sterilized porn, with technological wizardry,
has all the I-Bone boners
boning up on the fastest track to I-Boning.
It's the quickest quickie!
And the cyber, cerebral ejaculation,
is an anti-climactic mind fuck, to end all mind fucks.
The informazoas, as the software engineers,
have labeled them, are those little,
know-it polliwogs, just going absolutely nuts.
Impotence is the rage as the informazoas,
in a sterile solution, are off the charts.

The count, and then the recount, drops precipitously.
Falling off a cliff, is no fun,
especially when it comes to informazoas.
Everyone wants to be in the know
with their I-Bone.
Plug in and get groped, I-Bone style.
It's a loveless, candelabra-style,
Liberace I-Bone, shaped like
Gaga genitals; hermaphroditic,
zinger beats; ring blaster
from simulated, vas deferens, hardwiring.
The informazoans highway, is the one
everybody wants to ride.
Implanting is quick and easy.
The new I-Bone, 'infant procreator simulator,'
will have the I-Bone fetus, born invitro;
actually, right inside the I-Bone,
where that little critter will devolve
into a fully warped I-Bone.
No stretch marks. No contractions.
A surrogate I-Bone is the way to go.
Just look at 'Syrupy Puckered Farter'
from 'Sex with a Grid Iron,' a
steroidal enhanced I-Bone cretin.

Her ball sack is humongous,
supplanting her placenta,
which stores her surrogate,
cookie-cutter afterbirth, I-Boner.
The inventor, Hand Jobs, is mobbed
by the mobs of gobblers,
godhead of a headroom, a mouse-sized pecking order.
Capon of the hen house,
his I-Bone rules as cyber hatchlings sycophant.5
The I-Boning of Spamericans is the rage.
It's the desire of every, drudge-blooded Spamerican
to own their own I-Bone.
It's literally flying off the shelves.
The stores can't keep them in stock.

Once dialed in, the miraculous I-Bone
helps gonads grow brain cells.
Sexless technology, running the airwaves,
makes sexy techie passé.
Love is a thing of the past, with the I-Bone.
How many and how often
the insertions are needed, first and foremost, for getting off.

seaturtlenation@gmail.com

It was marketed by violentology
and El Don Hubbub.
It's a great marketing tool,
giving customers an opportunity
to have an informazoas count
and explore the possibilities of sterility.
There are no knock-offs of the I-Bone.

Spamerica

Crisscrossing both borders, are fences, made of fiber-optic, razor wire, which transmits a microwave signal, neutralizing anyone, entering, that circumscribed kill zone. The fences are punctuated with nuclear armed gates.

Sensors are positioned to detect intruders.

If anyone were to come within 1.2 meters of the fence,

a cadmium, cylindrical shield, would drop down,
onto the unsuspecting victim.
A highly irradiated, anti-matter, a positron charge,
would be released, instantly vaporizing,
whoever was in that cylinder.
The gaseous residue, would be solidified,
through a titration filament,
and then converted into a colorless, odorless, drudge cake.

A magnetic, imaging system
would hold the particles, in suspension for further use.

These were used, to replicate, spamatron generators:
four-dimensional, holographic projections
with the height-width-length configuration
built into the design.

The fourth dimension was almost an intangible.

A NEURMC (Nanosecond Ebot Unchanger Rubrics Metric Chip) sets parameters as a guidance coordinator.

A directional finder, recalibrated, to stay
within the confines of purpose;
a normal and manually manipulated,
monitored definition, unchanged.
This was the time line of the future,
in compliance with the fact-based,
informational highway of the past.
A mechanism that remained static.
The processing unit was engineered
for immutable duplication.
It was a virtual reality,
which had materialized, a parallel universe,
eclipsing the natural world.
Artifice and fake stratagem,
was at the core of Spamerica.
The obfuscation of the present was the objective.
Now (that is, the here and now, the present)
made it too painfully clear how out of sync
the humanures were.
It was not listed on the day timer.
That pain was too unexpected.

It did not fit. It did not belong to
anything that was considered important.
It never made the roster. There was no room for it.
Classified as unwanted and undesired,
pain had to be eliminated.
The two institutional methodologies
best suited for killing were the D.O.D. (Department of Drudgers) and the Medikill industrial complex.
Both killers, in their own right,
WMR (Weapons of Mass Religiosity)
and invasive procedures and painkillers, killed
for the sake of killing.
Based on skewed facts and hijacked information,
the agents of killing, operated based on an oxymoron:
killing in the name of fairness and justice.
Towering glass and steel enclosures,
manufactured the corporate policy for killing.
A killing, in the market is justifiable.
A killing, on the battlefield is heroic.
Civilian casualties escalate.
The death toll stat, is off the charts
and deliberately falsified.

The Spamerican franchise, had poisoned the waterholes. Innocent victims

drank Koke (El Don Hubbub's secret formula). The privatization of war and disease, were now publicly traded companies. The two were the biggest of big businesses. Unchecked behemoths, devouring everything and everyone; default swaps derivatives, connoting a broken system, pigging out ,on more slop, on the material wealth, that zeroes out, when they stick you in that box and push the button, that zeroes out as your incinerated remains, get permanently parked in the parking garage called hell.

Top heavy, corporate Buysauruses were geared to plunder and pillage and rob you blind. But the crime fit the punishment as bailouts were packaged sellouts. Legislated politicos sit opposite the mug shot line up of "bankster", slime balls.

Begging for a handout,
the white collar criminals,
headed up by Father Heist,
are codified rape artists:
churchy, preachy, creepy do gooders,
give the devil himself a bad name.
'Too Big to Fail,' greedy,

snake-eyed monstrosities, robbed and cheated.

It had to come. It was inevitable.

The crap shoot, hit a wall.

And the deck, stacked with aces of spades, collapsed. Toppling and tumbling in a deafening roar of obsolescence.

The underbelly, the foundation of hypocrisy and deceit,

would inevitably crumble and fall.

A cyber calendar is hooked up to

the virtual reality treadmill.

The gyroscopic balancing act runs

on the fumes of overdrive, fast tracking,

over-used, overworked, 'need to do' more, burn outs.

Mule doers cued up to self-absorb and misfire.

Piggy backing drudge,

the 'need to do' crowd,

is hollowed-out .

Spiraling out of control,

the overcooked, "need to do MORE", junky,

high on spoon-fed pabulum, goes from the grindstone

to the meat grinder.

Energy brown outs,

looking like chopped liver,

are not exactly what, you'd call 'the picture of health.'

Termination is not planned. It's definitely not on the calendar. There is no upside. It's all downside.

There are no perks as you zero out.

It becomes cliché and obsolete as your portable rattrap, crashes and burns.

The dual core operating system,
designed for fastest times,
gets the worms and crashes the system.
A frontal lobe motherboard,
had been implanted,
programmed and reprogrammed, a controlled supplanted need,
running off a hybrid synthesizer,
synthesizing doing and needing MORE,
at a rapacious rate; a controlled,
reckless, self-destructive, undisciplined rule book,
a time release capsule,
redundantly repeats and continues to repeat,
so the trauma of repetition,
will suffuse and supplant, the functional,

creative capacity of stress.

It then begins to degrade and breakdown.

The result, the glue that holds the whole thing together, fractional,

fragments and malfunctions.

The symptom-based, Medikill disease model, is employed. It codifies and victimizes, inside the problematical box. Tested and retested, with pathological accuracy, the victim is now diagnosable and prepped for victimization.

The formula—kill cut and invade—is set into motion. This is where the Medikill industrial complex, cashes in.

seaturtlenation@gmail.com

Lianetics

Angelips Jowly, long before she became a judge, she was and still is the Eva Braun of Spamerica. She is El Don Hubbub mistress.

He wrote science fiction books and gradually, devolved into being the author of Lianetics. He and Angelips Jowly hooked up years before the advent of Violentology. That kind of publicity, his affair with Jowly and having founded Violentology was what, catapulted him, into the spotlight.

It's become a global cult. Lianetics is the Violentology bible. It teaches, the violence of violence, a fallowed, bull horn, shock-scraper scraping of your remains off the back pages of blind obedience.

"The Module of Violentology, has become a global cult. Lianetics is the bible of Violentology. It teaches the violence of violence, a fallowed, bull horn, shock-scraper, scraping of your remains, off the back pages of blind obedience.

"The subcultural science of submission to Lianetics is subliminally induced violence. It's just below the radar. A Lianetics recharger is implanted, so your mind becomes like a mini nuclear reactor, producing robotic, angstrom, isotopic, radioactive heart stoppers, flattening out the heart's rhythm and shutting down the heart chakra.

"A built-in, retuning gets you to resonate at a violentology pitch of self-deconstruction; at the same time, it reconstructs you, into the image of El Don Hubbub: a bobble headed, self-serving, junky.

"Getting flunked, punked and junked, all at the same time; flunked at being you, punked for being exposed as a flunked and obviously junked, for failing the Lianetic litmus test.

"A frontal assault with
El Don Hubbub's testicular prosthetic implant
as a hind-brain operative, the mechanically, humanoid,
over wound, redundancy, replayed, rerun,
broken record subtext,
in voluminous, Lianetic syntax,
spelling out, a gutted space,
where you once, had a heart and a soul,
replaced with prefabricated,
El Don Hubbub vocal cords,
so you can be a rep dub of his simulated voice.

"They heart becomes a bagger,
bagging the junk box brain,
with over reactive informazoa,
flooding the informazoan highway,
Lianetic, battery-operated,
over-amped informazoas,
stream electronically.
It's an El Don Hubbub jerker controller.
It's a technical white out, simulating a blizzard,
where static screens simulate and replicate.
You can't see your hand, in front of your face,
but it forecasts your future.
Minds are replaced, with empty appendages,
filled with piss-colored kihl,
bringing out the killer in you.
A left brain jerks off, with an atrophied,
peanut-sized right brain, shrunken from disuse.
It becomes a left brain. Power grid
a one-sided, fact-based informazoan highway.
It's all about control.
Violentologist terrors goosestep
to the neo terrorists of El Don Hubbub's one dimensional module.

“That’s shocking news,” Ungohdt says. “I had no idea of the extent of El Don Hubbub’s empire. And he most recently aligned himself with Elvis Judas Krist to pull off the most diabolical, hostile takeover, in history. They have President Oblaba shaking in his boots.”

The Poetry of "Not-Know",

In the middle of his rainforest at his own Theatricum Botanicum, a small clearing, surrounded by, majestic non trees, with his audience of one, his faithful companion Dohg, he recites his latest poetry, "The Poetry of Not-know".

"We are born into not-knowing.
A breathless, lifeless knower, not-knows.
It just is.
An explorer is, an atomic reefer,
finding madness, in the fine print, of order.
The smoky film of nothing imprints.
Footprints and hand prints, on chalk boards, reminisce. The unremembered of memory lane,
implores the intruder.
An inviter calls. Destiny sets sail.
Homer's sirens wail.
Emptiness listens.
Naught is triumphant.
Placed in a sea of subtexts,
the physics of displacement,
in a sea of presumptions,
sinks from the weightiness of presuming.
Answering, folly is the fall guy,

the clown, the fool, a dreamer,

lost in the wake.

The errant majesty, of not-knowing, concedes.

A cosmic firmament is placed, on a carousel, of universes. Chaos kneads and tosses.

The dough of time is baked.

The outcome is convivial.

Playing is the groove.

A magical, make believer, personifies.

Unpracticed innocence simply plays.

A shapeless purveyor juggles.

The nova of a dream bursts.

Who is the un-knower of all things?

Un-knower and guesser/player, interchange.

They couple intimately, in play.

The manifestation of change becomes apparent.

Why change? Asking why is implicit.

It allows change, to change. It is an exercise in existence.

It is, therefore it exist.

A temporal moment explodes.

Now, fosters change.

Now, only in now, without a past or future comports change.

Day, becomes night and night becomes day,

is a pathless path

A changer, somehow, becomes the instrument.

All tomorrows, employ today.

The calendar of change,

invisible to the naked eye,

sees through a knower

and hears through a listener,

engaging in an orgy of the senses.

It's the sexiest thing imaginable.

Never becoming, the coming, climaxes,

into a dawn or nightfall or the empty stare of emptiness glistens, under a rogue moon.

The implication of creation reflects.

The invisibility of unknowing, casts a long shadow. Measured in light years, the calendar disassembles.

The proverbial yardstick, catapults.

And so change calibrates.

A stagnant pool re-energizes.

A fresh stream infuses consciousness.

Colder than ice, it freezes time.

The end wall, blocks. A writer circumvents.

Rewriting the panorama,
in horizons of majesty, is sequential.
Streaming consciousness draws from the well of unconsciousness.
Knower and the plebe recounts.
Summits, bottom out.
Cliff hangers become cave dwellers.
The bed of roses, is the top soil.
A river bottoms richness.
Wastelands, become wetlands.
Wildlife flourishes. Feathers of death, alight.
The great condor of the cosmos, feeds on carrion. Planetary carcasses, on the savannah,
are devoured and recycled.
Droppings warmed, by a temperate climate,
move through the bowels of an earth,
to be deposited on, the surface of a desolate plain.
A Bode tree begins as a seed,
in the warm piled excrement, of a forager.
It germinates.
Roots grow downward, into the subsoil,
past the alluvial wash of bygone ages,
through the fossilized stratum,

of nonexistence, into the aqua firs,
well springs fed by vestal streams.
Silt drifts. Fallow fields are nourished.

Fertility burst into bloom. Species self-materialize. Evolution wheels through time.

The core of spontaneity, erupts.
Stampeding elephants, trample.
The trunk of ultra-consciousness, can be tactile.
Hundreds of muscles, lift a peanut,
a glowing star, a grain of salt.
Instinctual, it digs a wellspring.
Does not-know, the digger?
The thinker, is mute.
Deafer than a door knob, it hears a pin drop.
Pinhead stars, on a rhinestone bronco,
bucks and kicks and finally is broken,
by the order of things.

Ultra-consciously, unaware of a conscious speck, unexplained, unedited, uncensored,

the freedom of now sparkles.
In a wilderness, survival finds its footing.
From the slowest, to the swiftest, infuse.
From dissolution, to evolution, herds migrate.
Down an escarpment, headlong, they stampede.

Playing out, an instinct for survival,
is the basis of prehistoric.,
Up an embankment,
following a migratory route,
the imprinting tracks.
The roaring cataract foams, white waters froth.
A rock python uncoils. A rain forest hisses.
The steamy everglades,
pervades wildly untamed.
An alligators jaw, slams shut.
The death roll, rips and tears and dismembers.
A reptilian appetite, for survival, consumes.

The instinct is fed.
A shredder undresses.
Anew, rapture plays dissonance.
Hyena laughter is, spine tingling.
Tear's of a clown, saddens the maker.
Fear and courage,
pathos and ethos measure, a thimble full.
The swifter the runner,
the greater chance, for survival, is merely a precept.

A tortoise is has the instinctual wisdom, engaging in not-knowing, whose shell, holds both, the treasure chest and the key.

Slowing to a screeching halt, a hare spins, on its heels.

The racer of doing becomes undone.

The pacer triumphs, undoing. And so the winner is supplanted by the loser.

And lost, bows to found, coalescing into the instigator,

who is the inquisitor of "what's happening",

in an ensemble. It's music to the ears of a millipede. Whose thousand legs,

play, a thousand different rhythms?

In reply, to a thousand different hearts,

the symphony crescendos.

In a thousand different ways,

surrounded by a thousand different rays.

It multiplies into infinity.

Clawing its way into being,

from the endless, infinity begins now.

A portrait of a faceless sage, mirrors.

A larvae caterpillar will spin its chrysalis.

A galaxy butterfly lilts.

Lifespan, into ageless unknowns, beget knows.

Red sockeye, instinctual battle, against the current, upstream they spawn.

The circa illuminates, plays on, under a canopy of assumptions, playing to the choir, conducted by a provocateur. Whose net is cast?

Reeling in, transference is unreal.

Discarded hopes, abandoned by hopelessness,

wait on the banks of the river,

timeless, fishing for bass or treble,

sharps and flats, the transcription of a musical score, superimposes.

The inscriber savant,

found genius, in not-knowing.

Hooks and tackle, attached to a line spiral.

An ebony whale vaults.

The white heron swoops.

Magic transpires.

A transaction is a worker bee's passion.

Gathering pollen sets the gold standard for splendorous instinct.

An exercise in survival is observed.

Caught by accident, "be amazed fascinated and wonder constantly."

Depressions sinkhole, is medicines bailiwick,
Killers shut down. A windowless box, is locked, by the Timekeeper, jailer.
Prosecutors of victims are victimized.
The industry of victimization enslaves.
No way in, no way out, is a death sentence.
Gridlock is a war of stalemates.

Cell block reality inters.
Dead end's implant, obsolescence,
jamming the connection: Submitters comply.
Prophylaxis distorts.
Invasive cutters saw through, a complacent sternum. Chests are ripped open, livers are transplanted.
Criminals, in white coats, violate.
Politico mules, like mosquitoes, in a swamp, infect,
passing on the disease process.
Blind eyes and deaf ears line up.
Shot uppers, affirm stupidity.
The mind of physicality,
sheds light on omnipotence.
Calling the inquirer, into play,
is the essence of why.
Inquiry is the hands and fingers, of the observer.

It's unknowing, the mold to reshape, what is.
The spiritual master of timelessness emerges.
A purveyor, is spiritually founded, in not-knowing.
Like a mythical dragon, it breathes fire.
Raven wings, the length of a universe, glide.
Updrafts soar. Downdrafts collide.
The invention of time,
suns into arms and faces.
Do the math.
Zero minus zero adds up to…
A borderless, conjugal unison becomes.
Seeded knowledge is born,
from the flower of not knowing.
Conversely, seed becomes flower.
Inversely, an intertwining sheds.
Communion is inevitable.
It's a balancing act, in midst of
unprecedented chaos.

Order is knowledgeable, not knowing.

Together, a gyroscopic universe, finds synchronicity. Magnets pull. Polar opposites attract.
A directionless metaphor perches.
A soundless galaxy proclaims.
A not-knowing pinwheel,
in a windless tunnel, suddenly spins.
Knowledge, whiling away,
not knowing, is the silent progenitor, of the stillness. Perfectly still, is the perfect storm.
Not knowing how, but at the same time knowing why.
This is empirical.
Unknowing, has knowledge of its unknowing.
A lion’s roar, brings not knowing,
into the predatory instinct, of instinctively knowing.
Purposeless, disassociates,
the material foundation of why it is here.
Why it is here, gives substance.
Knowing, without knowing is conducted.
The conduit is a wireless terminal.
The signal is a beacon. It’s a calling.
Who summons what?
A cleaner, wipes the slate clean.
Cleaner of who, knows what’s what?
Please identify cleaner.
A non-force, non-entity is enforcer.
It draws power from the anti-powered.
Meteorites, like scrap iron, is melted into nothing,
the sweeper is, the cleaner.
Superintendent of an undefined space,
a senseless parade, traveling through spheres.
The invisible broom and dust pan,
moves in a mindless sweep,
cleaning the glassless lens, of a looking glass,
stares blankly.
Rainbows go to black.
The theater of the inevitable, is chained to,
a shattered timepiece.

It's all for naught.
Rusted hinges, on an unhinged door, is left ajar.
A hint, shines into blindness.
Light, filters through.
Dustless swaths are squeaky clean.

A mender inter-meshes. The sender vies.
Who will proclaim victory?
The defeater or the defeated parry repost,
an unequaled dueling match.
Who will console everything?
Not knowing, is an empty, powder keg.
Knowledge, of the fuse, lights a potential.
Dead or alive, finds the redeemer
Antagonists unveil.
The explosive force, of implosion, is detonated.
A traveler rides it out. A builder reconstructs.
From deconstruction, great forests are built out of wastelands.
The society of want ascribes.
It knows what it desires.
As the ballasts of unwanted and undesired,
keep the ship afloat, somehow, dropping anchor.
What is the glue? Glued parts?
Implausible wholes rectify?
Braced by solitude, the stormy seas convulse.
I'm on a roll?
As a wavelength of not-knowing,
redefines me, I meander.
No straight lines here.
No defining moments.
Reinvention is laborious.
I just wing it, hopelessly.
Why chance it? It's too simple.
The carriage postures and bends.
The workings of a whole, dives in,
belly flops, into a pool of parts.
Actually, it's an ocean,
which slaps up against, my hull

and sinks me into the raging depths.
Who knows what?
Cut loose and just drift! Figure it out!
It's easy and simple.
Talking to me, is a universe unto itself,
with countless lifetimes, cultures,
an ageless raconteur, provocateur,
the worst of the worst teaser,
a Bali Hi dreamer,
shipwrecking me, on an island of, unanswered questions.
Fear hits me, like a wrecking ball.
Not knowing consumes me.

The heads of Wilber and Dyer,
sit propped up, on the shore.
I'm an actor like Tom Hanks,
in the movie Castaway.
Imagine being stranded, on an island,
looking at those, coconut shaped heads,
staring back at me.
Hairless, bald, erudite, pundits,
bodiless prevaricators, skimming the surface,
referential shallows, Tao to Tao seconds, quote.
Heartless Zen benders,
roll along the shoreline,
catching the wave of self-denial and apathy,
feeding on the inadequacies of out of gas,
junkies and their own impotency.
From a single strand, the hair splitting begins.
A whole, becomes the sum of its parts.
The black hide of eternity, is smooth as silk.
Ides twinkle.
Seeing is not-believing, tethered to, not knowing.
Blinding knowledge is, an all seeing orb.
Planets orbit and moons revolve.
A listener gazes.
A cart blanch, implying unknowns,
gets Zebra Stripes and hooves.
Galloping heeds no sign.

What a way, to camouflage,
an unchartered wilderness.
It's an airless jungle.
A treeless plain, without a horizon, begs the question.
Ends and beginnings end and begin,
at the origin of not knowing?
A knower scrambles, gambling, on 'the play'?
Who or what and whom of where,
becomes inconclusively undetermined.
When it will manifest, is as good a guess as mine?
A minefield of uterus's carries, to term,
fetuses of not-knowing.
The limitless suckles.
An ageless Faustian saint, births the heavens.
Heavens upon heavens becomes a ladder,
a spiraling stairway,
to halcyon, hellish ambrosia.
The DNA of nothing,
unstrung beads, wander aimlessly.
It congruently adheres to incongruous.
That serpentine continuum is supplanted,
by a mismatch of futility and happiness.
Can they co-exist or does one eclipse the other?
Welcome ephemeral.
Seeing happier days is a legitimate reason, for nihilism.
That doesn't make sense,
but neither does, looking at the futile wail, of not knowing.
Knowledge transparently is the see through skin.
The wound up unwinding is sloughed off.
Outer becomes, the magnifier of inner.
Breaking down, the door is short lived.
Not knowing quivers. Now, a blank stare, pervades.
Here, greatness transcends.
The composition of the train of thought is a symphony.
Tracks meander. Derailed, an accident happens.
Rails reposition. It's full steam ahead.
An operator crisscrosses.
Mountains, bridges and rivers are confluent.
A symbiosis commutes the sentence, to life.

A dealer holds the ace of spades.
Restrung tightropes traverse the slopes.
The train ride is, never ending.
Always, is riveted, to the whole.
The builder waxes. The debt collector wanes.
The purveyor is, ties the knot.
A marriage of known and unknowns, consummates.
Who is the composer and why?
And why continue, to play?
A self-answered player of all questions unrelentingly asks. The play has written its own script.
A writer never writes, knowingly.
For the plurality of knowing,
enters, the endless vacuum, of not knowing.
Knowing, becomes the seedling,
growing into, an ageless, sequoia rooted, in not knowing.
One, cancels, the other out.
In a moment of sustained attraction,
now, illuminates a physical body.
From omniscience, to finite,
the seer and listener merge.
Impractically, perpetuating creation,
a maker, presses the flesh of the creator,
to extract a molded, anatomical wishing well,
to give dimension, to nothing.
Who holds the rose?
Fragrance strikes, the senses. Who will ever know?
Not knowing enters, the garden, to be tantalized.
Something, pounds relentlessly, a lob dub rhythm.
Sound, gives knowledge, to what is,
the deity of not knowing.
Now, if you are lost. Congratulate yourself.
Not knowing has lost its way,
winding through, the labyrinth of a cochlea.
Knowledge struck a nerve.
The synapse of not knowing, is the bridge,
between bliss and ignorance.
It is absolutely blissful, not knowing.
And so, the knowledge of ignorance,

replenishes and renews.
It has found shelter,
in the knowledge of being, completely enchanted,
by not knowing.
Being the sand of the Sahara dunes,
only answers, to the winds.
They come and go as they please.
Ignorant of direction,
they find a mind, to decipher and learn.
The dunes and a mind, share the bread of time.
It nourishes. It feeds an undying thirst.
A ravenous hunger howls. The endless orchestrates.
An oasis arises, from the emptiness.
Date palms, shade and water quenches the thirst.
The not knower parades,
a caravan of not knowing.
Winnowed grain, seeds the barrenness.
Chaff blows away,
fanned by a balmy breeze,
catching the fronds, dancing, to a desert rhapsody.
A hushed whoosh, finds solace,
in the knowledge of, not knowing.
Solitude, unmasks.
Rogue atoms, ignite the blaze.
Anti-energy, torches the sun dried,
sun bleached savannah.
Twisting on its axis,
    the white eyed celestial gleam,
beaming into the forecaster of anti-energy,
unleashes a black light, glimmering sheen,
a panther shaped, constellation,
crouched, ready to strike.
Dead silence, rules. Nothing is emperor.
Emptiness is vagabonding,
through the trackless tundra, of the unknown.
An unwashed traveler wanders.
A dustless trail, spirals, festooned in directionless.
A pathfinder, bridges the gap.
A binding and its book cover, hold no pages.

The book-less, unspoken, in a wordless text of unthinking, is voluminous.
How can it be? Who can it be?
Investigate the properties.
Bats, hanging, upside down,
in a cavernous prologue, defecate, where they live.
And countless, stalagmites, jut upward
Like bookmarks, they ring the floor.
Exclamations, are staggered.
Impaling, the blankness, is a mute, with no tongue.
A preeminent listener,
observes as a mountaintop listens,
to the sky, the unspoken, harbor of the heavens.
A voiceless bell ringer, in a black as coal steeple,
is crushed, under the weight of, ten trillion light years. Diamonds, in a windless tunnel,
are scattered. To intone magic,
the ceaseless ringing,
falls on the deaf ears, of the bell ringer,
who too, has risen from the dustless,
minefields of the eternal,
to be a chalky, white, translucent constellation,
hanging from, the outermost cliffs,
of a bottomless canyon.
From the ceiling, stalactites,
mineralization vamps, star studded and constellation vaporization.
A roofless Stonehenge, points to futility.
Nothingness remains. Alone, provides sanctuary.
Whispers haunt. All pervasive silence deafens. Backtracking, explains divine providence.
Stranded unknowns, chase the mystery.
From the Canary's to Betelgeuse,
a crossroads surfaces.
A flip of a coin, determines direction.
The two sides, are forged.
A questioner, answers the one.

The dust of cultures, past and present,
are scattered, to the windless, endless, still.
A juggler hurls stalagmites,
like a knife thrower, at a circus.
And the Promethean stalactites reconfigure, into a passageway, lit by Diogenes' torch.
A mime gestures and suggests.
Who can know, whether it is a clown
or fool or jester, that has taken shape and form?
A lost vagrant finds poetry,
in the empty pockets of humility.
The grand gesture of a humbler knower,
bows to, an all pervasive, dazzler, not-knowing.
Prostrations, to a cosmic art form,
seems inconsequentially formless.
A multitudinous canvas is painted,
by broad brush strokes.
Wrapped around sinew and bone,
the anatomy of being is framed.
Muscle and grit, shear through, the gravity of reality.
A time keeper, fine tunes the instrument.
The Stradivarius is bowed, by a progeny.
An ageless prodigy reinvents.
Genius plays on.
The invincibility of not knowing,
is both, paradoxical and paradigm.
The cliché, “science is knowledge”,
is rebuked by not-knowing.
Progenitors, know-er and not-know-er bridge, an expanse, non-degrees of separation,
not knowing, has no knowledge, of not knowing.
The river is the caretaker of the knower,
whose knowledge,
like a sculptor's hammer and chisel,
carves great gorges and waterfalls,
in answer to, unknown inquisitiveness.

It is implicit.
It suggests and at the same time questions.
It is unreasoning at its best.
It is unintelligible.
There is no design.
The purse strings of chaos and order,
are pulled together, by not-knowing.
The fabric of not-knowing is the naked truth.
"I" found, "me", in not knowing.
"Me is I, to acknowledge we."
The species being, listens to instinct.
Survival teeters on, extinction.
The climate of change rules timelessness.
Adapting is critical.
The collective bargaining power of we, surmounts.
To reach and stretch, entreats.
An accident happens.
Reason, is thrown out the window.
A ticking time bomb, quantifies.
Non-existence implodes, into denounced existentialism.
An arbitrator of randomness, conducts.
Mozart's teacher resides.
A transcriber mines.
Nouns mime, the actor.
Where are you going with this?
Why ask? Does it really matter?
Gravitas, becomes a weightless boomerang.
Matter and antimatter, annihilate,
The annihilator becomes creator.
Artist inimitable draws creation.
Finding art, with an unlit light, is a counterpart.
Here, now, art exhibits.
Hanging, in a gallery of not-knowing,
an implausible cosmos, looms.
It found a pulse.

The lifeless corpse comes alive.
A fetal state, positions the incomparable.
Smooth surfaces become contiguous.
One breathes into the other.
Functionality, depends on the interplay.
Who is the breather?
And what is the drawer?
And who is the founder?
And where is the discoverer?
As the adventurer, risks everything,
to plunge into, nothing,
the tug of war, becomes a treatise, for peace.
How hallowed? A rotted out tree hollow,
holds the secret, to dead standing.
Whose forest, is from a loom?
Who or whom, is the weaver?
The fabric of unknowing,
threads the knower needle, serendipitously.
It's always by chance.
And never, is the threadbare, stumble bum.
Shouldering night, his pathless quest mazes,
The dance troupe, crowds the dance floor.
They wander off.
Meandering footsteps pitter- patter, inquisitively.
Not knowing rains down.
A measureless storm, gathers around the eye.
Calm electrifies. Quiet confronts.
The palpable antagonism drifts.
The dichotomy, verges on the not-know-er.
Dualities duel, dusk to dawn. A single note transcends.
Pretenders, pretend to know.
Pundits, punting the ball of self-aggrandizement,
Self-absorb. Tenders of the goal, lose sight.
The ultimate corrector makes the final decision.
Gamers game, each other.

Dinosaurs of a self-absorbed age, self-destruct
Zen qualifiers, preoccupy.
They plagiarize.
Copycats, defenders, self-promulgate.
Carbon copy offenders, violate the sanctity.
Wholeness becomes, hellishly compliant to fractions.
    Preachers of wholeness, with fork tongues, snake.
A catatonic whole, fragments.
The puzzler teaches puzzlement.
Questions are deluded?
Masks are referential.
The strangler deletes impending.
So now as the searcher, live by your mistakes.
Where is this going? Does it really matter?
A good dose of cynicism, remedies the drudgery.
The lumbering generics, intrude.
Indexes, are incomplete wholes,
attached to the preachers,
the A to Z panderers of the Tao,
who get lost, in complacency.
Disinformation is reformulated.
The complacent, proctors, disseminate.

Informers squeal, uniformly.

Snitches brag. Jailed factors employ factitious imposition.

How do you, make sense, out of the whole thing?

Where is this going?

No sense, nonsense or possibly uncommon sense?

The odds are stacked.

For and against, lean against each other,

in a monolithic, towering obelisk.

The crowning achiever waives indifference.

Monuments to power, collapse,

under their own weight.

They are on a plane of encroachment.

Having outlived their usefulness, they disintegrate.

The culture of submission dissolves.

Entombed edifices gobble up huge portions of the sky, providing a haven for the spreadsheets of reinforced concrete and steel,

built glass houses, jut upward.

A plain of consciousness unconsciously eludes.

Twin truths, absolute and relative, contrive.

Contrivers, manage egos.

Absolute power corrupts absolutely.

The death toll, consumes humanity."

seaturtlenation@gmail.com

The sun has set, the heavens are sparkling, with what, looks like a field of diamonds. Ungohdt finished his poem and arm in arm with his sidekick Dohg, they call it a night and go into their forest home to prepare for the next chapter in their tireless efforts to help save the natural world.

seaturtlenation@gmail.com

Jimmy Wrhongman

"My name is Jimmy Wrhongman. I was born on the wrong side of the tracks. Yep, that's right. My parents are Cecilia Mystake and Virgil Wrhongman. My mother is still alive. She's almost one hundred and one and my father is deceased.

I was hit, by a lightning bolt, when I was two and a half years old. It struck me, on the top of my head, so my hair frizzed and is pure white and nappy, on one side and straight and pure black, on the other side.

I'm from a little town called, Dreamscape. It borders on the virtual reality border of Whad Street, a cyber-spaced extension of walled up, boarded up, Wall Street, a wadded up, spit ball, ghost town, shot full of entrances and entryways, going nowhere, riveted with gridlocked ramps, misfiring, disinformation highways, coming off a blackout grid, leading to a multitude of dead ends.

Believe it or not, with absolutely no exits, no way out, a maze like seize-way, crisscrossing the market share battlefield, digitized, in high definition, like a strangulated, series of varicose veins, hanging onto the gangrenous, ''last leg",

Inextricably bound to a virtual reality treadmill, super mousetrap, a gutted tower, stands as a monument to an upended slough, murky debacle, shattered and broken, having fallen into abject dissolution, a far cry, from its heyday brandishing it's brand, the BS-2 marquis of power and greed.

A pock marked war zone, covered over, with doorways, to boutiques, filled with shredded evidence, bits and pieces of what was, Bulls and Bears. The brutal carnage is like nothing you've ever seen. The virtual reality, meat grinder, has taken its toll, to say the least. Blood and gore, is not my cup of tea. I feel like I have been overexposed. I'm on sensory and visceral, overload.

I have seen earlobes, with tea bag, earrings. That's it, only earlobes and earrings! And tongues, with giant gold piercing, dollar signs, drilled into its center. That's it, only tongues, pierced! Nothing else, only tongues, no mouths nor bodies. Stomachs, the size of walnuts, with a band around them, that's all you could see. Oh yes, a ball sack without a penis, explain that one!! An ass, the size of a kitchen table, just lying, in the middle of the street, I swear you could have a breakfast on it. Get this, I came across, tattooed eyeballs, blood shot red, very freaky. On the eyeball itself, no socket and not any part of the face or head. And between, more bear rugs, than I can count and mountains of bull shit, I could definitely go into business, either selling bear rugs or selling bullshit. Pretty diversified, don't you think?

By the way, I met Ungohdt AKA Dr. Summon and Dohg a couple of weeks ago and I have decided, to help them out. One thing, Ungohdt hired me for, is to get Ungohdt's book out there, somehow market it. So I am standing here, with these cue cards as Ungohdt had asked me to do, (like Bob Dylan did, I followed his instruction, but I never heard of Bob Dylan. It must be before my time). And just keep shuffling, these cue cards for the theater crowd or whoever else comes along. Ungohdt told me, he and Dohg will be back, with another book or what he called, "the next installment", a continuation of his playbook. I guess this is the 'Introduction'. Its Ungohdts way of getting the word out there, to me it comes at you, like a bull in a china shop. And so here I am just helping out. Until the next time, I hope we meet again and maybe I'll get a chance, to clean up the mess, on WHAD STREET and maybe, Wall Street will be resurrected. Who knows? Maybe Ungohdt and Dohg have the answers. I'm just working for them temporarily.

seaturtlenation@gmail.com

The Final Devolution

On the north eastern end, of the island of North Spamerica, is the shanty town of Albya, where the last of the Manhattoes now live.

They are within ten miles of a nuclear power plant. The nuclear reactor, having high concentrations of plutonium, has gone through a serious meltdown, exposing the Manhattoes to high levels of radiations (one million times the normal dose).

Recently hit, with a terrifying tsunami, due to an offshore earthquake, 9.5 on the Richter scale (the largest in recorded history), the damage to the Manhattoe village and the nuclear reactor, was severe and worsening, each day as well as wiping out, a large number of Manhattoe Indians, who were swept out to sea. There bodies were not recovered.

The nuclear plant, NYRE (New York Radiation Exchange), has not been up

to code, for decades. The housing of the reactor, was breached. The concrete walls, are crumbling and the steel cover, is cracked, exposing the fuel rods. There is no fresh water, to cool them, the heat, from the reactor, rose alarmingly, giving off toxic steam, into the environment.

The inside traders and corporations like, Ghoulman Sacks, running the exchange, were paid, huge bonuses, to cover up, the leak. Matter of fact, they fixed the prices, on drugs, such as kihl, throwing gasoline onto the fire of over inflation. The big board, in many ways, was a reflection of unchecked, white collar crime. Inside trading, caused an inflationary firestorm. Terrorme Inc. and companies like Kihl International, skyrocketed.

Renewable sources of energy were obliterated. The radicalization of power and greed, morphed into an autocratic oligarchy. Somewhere between, a dense, radioactive miasma and invisible, toxic drudge, spewed out, into the atmosphere. When inhaled, it made the islanders, more unhealthy, agitated and more aggressive; more prone to addiction and self-destructive habits.

Once a proud, sovereign nation, the Manhattoes have lost their sovereignty. The corporate bullhorn, headed up by El Presidente "Crooked Don" T-Rump, El Don Hubbub, Judas Elvis Krist and President Oblaba, are currently in the process, through legal channels, are going to annex, that north eastern part of North Spamerica, including Albya.

In their backroom dealings, they are calling it, "The Final Devolution". It's a clandestine cabal; totalitarian rule, with militaristic, demagogic demonizing, a xenophobic, homophobic, over-consumption, the overdosing, over abusive leanings and fascistic brainwashing, emblematic of social decay and decadence. The herded masses are corralled, in a proxy state of overkill.

A sweetheart deal, unprecedented, which includes the eminent domain suit, is taking place. Fanning the hatemongering, BS-2 demagoguery, throws red meat to his walking dead. Also throwing gasoline on the fire, adds fuel to the warring factions, in a class action lawsuit, involving the southern tip of North Spamerica, where the twin towers once stood. Crooked Don, addresses his whipped up violent mob: "The only obstacle is Ungohdt and his sidekick Dohg, and that, so called rainforest of theirs. They must be destroyed! We must show them no mercy, take no prisoners, with the exception of the Masseuses of Avalon, who will become our prisoners, teaching them a lesson, they will never forget, letting them know, who we are and what we stand for!" His stereotypical loudmouthed rant, mirrors his hidden intent, purging, depopulating, a walled in, armed camp, so he can promote, his surreptitious, insidious isolationism, walling off his hired hackers, wall-ware virus. Vlad The Impaler, micromanages the hacking, trolling war footing invasion of the U$A. Like a cyberspace pinball video game, he invades, divides and conquers, while bitch slapping his puppet (downplaying what is fast becoming his puppet state).

El Presidente "Crooked Don" T-Rump signs off on, shit-canning Spamerica: "The Final Devolution."

Author: Dr. Blackman

seaturtlenation@gmail.com

Made in the USA
Columbia, SC
23 December 2022

74069309R00150